THE LITTLE-ASTWICK MYSTERIES (BOOK 2)

Grave concern at the Manor

C.S. Rhymes

Copyright © 2024 C.S. Rhymes

All rights reserved

The characters and events portrayed in this book are fictitious. Any similarity to real persons, living or dead, is coincidental and not intended by the author.

No part of this book may be reproduced, or stored in a retrieval system, or transmitted in any form or by any means, electronic, mechanical, photocopying, recording, or otherwise, without express written permission of the publisher.

Cover design by: C.S. Rhymes

For Mum & Dad

CONTENTS

Title Page
Copyright
Dedication
Prologue
Chapter one — 1
Chapter two — 6
Chapter three — 11
Chapter four — 22
Chapter five — 31
Chapter six — 43
Chapter seven — 53
Chapter eight — 67
Chapter nine — 77
Chapter ten — 101
Chapter eleven — 120
Chapter twelve — 129
Epilogue — 133

About The Author	137
Books By This Author	139

PROLOGUE

It was a bright sunny day, with a gentle breeze. Alan loved days like this, walking through the countryside, sweeping his metal detector gently from left to right and back again, feeling the warm sun on his face. Despite the warmth, he wore a lightweight waterproof jacket to protect him from the unpredictable English weather, along with quick dry walking trousers and walking boots with thick tread. He had a small rucksack on his back with various tools and a sandwich for his lunch.

On his head he wore his trusty baseball cap, covering his long hair that was pulled back into a ponytail, with his all important headphones over the top, covering his ears. He listened out for any beeps, announcing any metal in the earth twelve inches below his feet.

The field was just outside the village boundary of Little-Astwick. He could see the local pub a few fields away, with the church bell tower poking above the pub roof in the distance. In the other direction he could see the grand manor house of Manor Farm. He had already found an old nail and a beer can today, hoping that his luck would change.

Beep, beep, beep.

He stopped walking and swept his metal detector from side to side, confirming the exact location of the hit. He lowered to his knees and retrieved a narrow but fairly long shovel with serrated edges that was clipped onto his rucksack and began digging. First he carefully removed a square patch of the turf, using the serrated edge of the tool as a saw, so that he could replace it once he had finished. He then got out a wand metal detector out of one of his long pockets along his thigh, waving it around the area to better track the hit.

He removed some more soil, then waved the wand around, repeating the process over and over again until he spotted a coin. He picked it up and wiped away the grime, revealing a shiny surface underneath. He could already tell the value of the coin from the seven sides of the shape. He put the 50p coin into his pocket, thinking he might be able to buy a packet of crisps in the pub with it later in the day.

He waved the wand around the exposed earth and found another hit. He dug once more and this time it revealed a rectangular leather object. He pulled the object from the ground and brushed off the dirt.

It folded open and revealed itself as a wallet. There was a bank card with the name Steven Conrad. The card's expiry date was only last year. There was £20 cash and a few more coins in a small pocket, along with a library card with the name 'Evelyn McKenzie' printed in black ink.

Alan thought to himself that he had better try and find the owner of the wallet, but the £20 would buy himself a few pints of beer to go with his crisps, a just reward for making the discovery. He placed the wallet in his backpack, wondering how it could have got there in the first place.

He was about to replace the disturbed soil and turf top, but decided that it was worth waving the wand over one more time to double check there was nothing else. He swiped the wand side to side along the hole, from top to bottom. He had almost finished, but there was one more beep to be found.

A lucky hit.

He carried on digging. This time it took several attempts of removing soil and waving the wand before his next discovery was revealed, the hole now just over a foot underground. He probably wouldn't have found this third find without the two above to help indicate its location.

Another round metal shape appeared in the soil. He gently brushed off the soil with his fingers before removing his water bottle and pouring a little over the object to help clean it off. Despite the depth of the hole, the bright sunlight glinted the colour gold back at him.

Suddenly more excited he kept digging with his hands, after clipping his digging tool back into place on his backpack. It looked like a gold coin, about the size of a one pound coin. "Yes!" he shouted out loud. He wrapped his fingers around the coin and pulled it up, releasing it from the surrounding mud. Something suddenly felt very wrong.

He turned his hand over so the palm was facing upright, his fingers wrapped around the object. He slowly opened his fingers, revealing the coin to actually be a signet ring. Inside the ring was a bone.

A human finger bone.

He dropped the ring and bone back into the hole, stood back up and then ran back to the village as fast as he could, leaving his prized metal detector where it lay on the grass.

CHAPTER ONE

"Hello?" answered Evelyn's voice, sounding sleepy like she had just woken up.

"It's David, I need your help again!" David began.

"I know I said keep in touch, but you are coming across as a bit needy calling me the very next day!" joked Evelyn.

David chuckled, his tension draining away slightly. "Well, you remember in the underground room at the church, when I stubbed my toe?"

"Oh yeah, that was quite funny wasn't it?" Evelyn laughed.

"No, that's not what I mean." The tension was building within David now. He was so excited to share his news that he just blurted it out. "I found something under the raised stone. A leather cylinder. I forgot all about it after the relief of the door unlocking and then the encounter with Michelle!"

"What! How could you not tell me?" Evelyn gasped.

"Well, I'm trying to tell you now, but things happened and I forgot, and now you're joking and then shouting and…" David mumbled incoherently.

"Deep breath David!" Evelyn interrupted.

David stopped talking and took a deep breath. He was always less confident when he was out of the community support officer uniform. When he put it on it made him feel more sure of himself. It reminded him that he had earned the right to wear it by completing his training.

"Thanks Evelyn." David was feeling calmer once more after the support from his new friend. He cleared his head and began to speak clearly once more. "Right, I found the cylinder in my jacket pocket this morning. I saw a loose thread and gently pulled it. The string came away and the lid was free. I pulled the lid off and looked inside and there was…"

Beep, beep.

He looked down at his phone, there was another call coming in from his head office.

"Sorry, I've got to go. I'll call you back." David rushed, before ending the current call and accepting the new call. He could hear Evelyn shouting his name in anger before the call ended.

"Hello, David Morgan speaking." answered David.

"Good morning, Detective Inspector Barksley has requested your immediate presence at Manor farm, Little-Astwick." the robotic-like dispatch voice ordered.

"Yes, um, I mean affirmative. Understood." David replied.

"You are also required to bring a Miss Evelyn McKenzie with you." the voice finished.

"Evelyn? What for?" David asked.

"Please confirm." the monotone voice replied.

"Affirmative. Understood." David confirmed, then the call ended abruptly.

What does DI Barksley want, he questioned? Was it about yesterday's events? He hadn't even started writing up the report yet. He couldn't want that already? More to the point, what did he want with Evelyn too?

He redialled Evelyn's number on his mobile phone. She answered within two rings.

"You need to work on your manners. You can't leave someone in suspense like that!" Evelyn screeched.

"I'm sorry, but I've got to go to work and I need you too! I'll be at your house in twenty minutes so you had better get yourself ready." David ordered as politely as he could to his friend. "We can catch up later. I promise."

He hung the phone up before she could respond, then started getting dressed in his uniform, preparing himself for whatever the day had in store for him.

Chloe entered the white tent. Her hair was tied up into a bun to keep it out of the way. She was wearing her white oversuit to prevent her from contaminating the scene, her hood covering her hair, her overshoes covering her boots. She had gloves on her hands, with a dictaphone in her left hand.

Danielle now entered the tent, wearing a matching outfit.

Chloe clicked the record button, then said the date and time, slipping the recording device into her pocket, before saying her and Danielle's names.

"Officer Danielle Thompson and Doctor Chloe Harrison present at the scene." Chloe said.

"So what do we have here then?" Danielle asked.

Chloe started describing the scene.

"A uniform hole around 30cm square,

approximately 30cm deep, no sign of the tool used to create the hole at the scene. There is a gold ring with a phalange inside it at the bottom of the hole." Chloe took out a brush from her suitcase and started brushing away soil from the ring and the bone.

Danielle picked up a camera from one of the many boxes of equipment in the tent and started taking photos of the scene, zooming in close on the ring once Chloe had removed most of the soil.

They continued their work with patience and precision, treating the bones with respect.

CHAPTER TWO

David pulled his bike over, signalling he was slowing down by waving his right arm up and down slowly to the side. He followed his cycle proficiency training to the letter, despite there being no other road users in his immediate vicinity.

He wheeled his bike to Evelyn's front door and knocked. The door was answered promptly. She was standing at the door waiting for him to arrive.

She opened the door a few inches before saying, "Nope, try again!", then shut the door again with a gentle slam.

David stood there for a few seconds, bemused. He smiled to himself as he realised what was going on.

"Police! Open up!" David shouted, then started banging on the door loudly with his fist.

The door opened all the way this time and Evelyn stepped out. David chuckled to himself.

"That's better!" Evelyn smiled back at him. "That will give the neighbours something to talk about!"

She shut the door behind her and locked it, before turning to face David. She was wearing a lightweight, black, waterproof jacket with leggings and her walking boots. Her brown hair was tied up into a ponytail today with no need for a hat with today's sunshine warming up the morning.

She looked at David. He was wearing his community support officer uniform again, the same as the previous day. His hair was a little unkempt, sticking out a bit from under his hat. She assumed he probably didn't have time to go through his normal grooming routine due to the phone call.

"So, where are we going in such a hurry?" Evelyn asked.

"I'm actually glad you asked. Do you know where Manor farm is? I was in such a rush I didn't get a chance to look at a map. We need to meet DI Barksley there." David replied.

"Manor farm? Yes, it's just outside the village. A few minutes walk." Evelyn said. She pointed in the direction they had to go and they began walking, David wheeling his bike beside him.

"No Charlie today?" David asked, wondering where Evelyn's dog was.

"Unlike some people, I get up early everyday and take Charlie out for a walk. It gives me time to wake up and get ready for the day ahead. I even have time to brush my hair." Evelyn answered with a smile, David lifting his hat and smoothing his unkempt hair back under it before placing the hat back on his head. "So, what did you find?"

"Oh, yes." David, suddenly remembering how their phone call had ended. "I opened up the cylinder and there was more paper inside. It looked old and yellowed like the paper we found yesterday. Maybe it's a clue?"

"Maybe it's a clue?" Evelyn questioned, then stopped walking and stared at David. "You mean you haven't even looked at it yet?"

"Well, I…" he paused, his cheeks going red, suddenly feeling very shy. "I wanted us to look at it together."

The look of confusion on her face was replaced with happiness. She took a step closer to David and gave him a big friendly hug. David hugged her back. It lasted no more than two seconds before Evelyn stepped back and carried on walking. David carried on after her, quickly catching up.

"Ok, let's get this thing with DI Barksley out the way and then find somewhere to take a look at what you have found." She said excitedly. David nodded in agreement.

They walked the rest of the way, making small talk about the weather, the way British people do to pass the time. Their conversation was easy, able to chat freely, despite only meeting the previous day for the first time. They left the village, taking a footpath opposite the pub. A tall hedge was directly ahead, the footpath winding around it to their right.

Once they passed the hedge they could see the manor house of Manor farm in the distance, a couple of fields away. It was three stories tall, with tall glass windows designed to let in the daylight all year round. There were large chimneys picking out of the top of the grey slate roof. The walls were built from large dark brown ironstone blocks with limestone highlights around the windows and doors.

The house backed onto some gentle green hills that faded into the distance, the view from the top floor windows of the house must have been magnificent. But what caught their eye right now was the scene in front of the house.

Three police vans, two police cars and a small white tent in the field next to the house, with a police tape cordoning off the wider area.

They looked at each other, confused as to what the storm of activity was that they were walking into.

Inside the white tent, Chloe and Danielle both brushed away the dirt, working as a team, one on the many hand bones, the other slowly revealing the multitude of wrist bones.

Danielle, working on the wrist, finally uncovered some clothing.

"What do you recon about this?" Danielle asked Chloe.

"Cream, maybe originally white material. Probably linen." Chloe started. "The cuff of the shirt looks old, perhaps…" Chloe stopped talking and looked at Danielle. They didn't have to say a word to each other, but each knew what the other was thinking.

"Yes, I'm glad we both agree on this. I thought I was going crazy for a minute there." Danielle replied, relief showing in her voice. "I think I need to update Barksley."

Danielle stood up and left the tent, making a beeline for the large van parked outside, her white oversuit rustling as she walked.

CHAPTER THREE

They approached the police tape and stopped to look at the scene. Several people in white oversuits were hovering around the white tent, bringing in equipment from the vans parked nearby. There were a few officers in uniform securing the scene. One looked over at the new arrivals by the tape and started approaching.

"Good morning. Can I help you?" the officer shouted over as he walked closer to them. Once he was a few steps away, David recognised him as Officer Smith, the same officer that was at the scene of the church the previous day.

"Good morning Officer Smith." David replied back. The man approaching looked confused, not sure how they knew his name. David wasn't surprised as the officer barely looked at them yesterday before they were shooed away with contempt.

David thought he had better explain why they were

there before they were shooed away once more. " We have been called here by DI Barksley. Is he here? I am David Morgan and this is Evelyn McKenzie."

The police officer retrieved his notebook from his pocket and confirmed the names he had written down earlier.

"Ah, Mr Morgan and Miss McKenzie." Officer Smith said, before lifting the tape so they could step under. He pointed towards one of the vans that was larger than the others, then without saying another word, he walked off back in the direction he had come from, leaving them standing alone once more in the field. The pair looked at each other, confused as to why Officer Smith didn't escort them there himself. David would have also checked their ID to verify their identities. Obviously Officer Smith had more important things to do. They started to walk towards the van Officer Smith had pointed to.

The van was taller than the others, as well as wider. It had the police logo plastered on the side as well as the text 'Incident support', not forgetting the usual high visibility stripes and blue lights on top. There was a hinged side door that was closed, a small step had been pulled out from the side of the van to allow easier access to the raised door. They approached the side door and could hear someone shouting from inside.

David leant his bike on the outside of the van then knocked gently on the van door. The shouting voice suddenly dropped in volume, before shouting "Yes?".

David opened the door and looked into the van, the interior much darker than the daylight outside. There was a row of screens along the opposite side of the van with a small desk below running the length of the van and two chairs for operators to sit. A figure started walking towards the open door from the back of the van, his long coat swaying with the movement. He had a mobile phone in his hand, which he quickly slipped into his jacket pocket. As he moved into the light from the door, David and Evelyn recognised the face of Detective Inspector Barksley.

"Come in and shut the door behind you!" DI Barksley ordered, before walking towards the rear of the van once more. David entered first before glancing over his shoulder to see Evelyn following and then shutting the door behind her. Their eyes took a few seconds to adjust to the semi-darkness inside the van, the low level ceiling lights providing only minimal lighting to help any operators see the screens easier.

DI Barksley turned around to face them, dark rings showing below his eyes, accentuated by the lighting inside the van. His designer stubble was slightly longer than the previous day.

"David, I'm happy for you to observe here, but I need you to remain out of this. You are here as a courtesy."

DI Barksley said. He pressed a button on the side of the van, a small red light appearing next to it. He then turned to Evelyn and started reading her rights.

David and Evelyn stood in shocked silence. David wanted to ask what was going on, opening his mouth ready to ask his question, before DI Barksley scorned him, raising his finger to his lips to indicate he should remain silent.

"Evelyn McKenzie, do you know a Mr Steven Conrad?" Barksley asked.

Evelyn was still in shock, unsure whether to answer or not after the police caution. She looked at David, who shrugged, unsure what to suggest. She looked back at DI Barksley, the intense look in her eye made her mind up. She had nothing to hide and wanted to stand her ground.

"Yes, he was my fiance." Evelyn responded.

Barksley noticed the use of past tense with the word 'was'. He pondered over whether this meant more than it first seemed. "And when did you last see him?" Barksley barked back.

"Not since the day we split up. He left me the day we were speaking to the vicar to arrange our wedding. He walked out on me at the vicarage and by the time I got back to my house he had packed up his stuff and left." She could feel her heart beating in her chest, her eyes starting to water with tears, the raw emotions from that day coming back to the surface. Why was he asking her this, what did it have to do with the police? "Why do you want to know?"

DI Barksley paused, taking in the emotion on Evelyns face, trying to read whether she was telling the truth. Deciding if they were real tears of emotion or the act of a well prepared fraudster. He picked up a clear plastic bag from the long desk, under the screens, and held it up so she could see it more clearly.

"Recognise this?" Barksley asked, before adding a statement for the recording "I am now showing Miss McKenzie exhibit A."

Evelyn looked at the bag. It contained an opened leather wallet, displaying some bank cards and a library card. She saw the name 'Steven Conrad' on the bank cards before reading her own name on the library card. She reached her right hand towards the bag to take a closer look, but DI Barksley pulled it away before she could touch it.

"This is evidence in our enquiry. You are not allowed to touch it." DI Barksley put the bag back down on the desk. "I repeat, do you recognise it?"

"Well, it looks like Steven's wallet." Evelyn answered.

"So can you explain to me why Steven's wallet was found next to a dead body?" DI Barksley questioned, his face waiting expectantly for the answer.

"What? A dead body?" Evelyn was confused. She paused thinking what to say next, then continuing. "No, I can't explain that?"

She suddenly had a realisation. "It's not Steven is it?".

DI Barksley looked at her, taking in her body language, trying to decide whether she was lying or not. His instincts told him that she was telling the truth, but he deliberately waited longer than needed before talking again, a part of him enjoying the power he had when questioning suspects. He finally spoke, breaking the silence.

"Our investigations are continuing…" DI Barksley said before the side door to the van suddenly opened, spilling light into the room.

A person wearing a white oversuit, face mask, gloves and shoe covers entered the van. They pulled the hood off their head, revealing blonde hair tied up neatly, then removing the face mask.

DI Barksley looked extremely annoyed at the unplanned interruption. He spoke in an angry, but clear tone, for the benefit of the recording.

"Officer Danielle Thompson has entered the room." DI Barksley looked at the woman who had entered, then continued. "With what I hope is something extremely important!"

Danielle didn't even bother looking at Barksley, she looked straight at Evelyn, placing her gloved right hand out for a handshake, before quickly withdrawing her hand and taking the glove off with her other hand, then putting the hand back out for another handshake.

"Officer Danielle Thompson, forensics." She smiled at Evelyn. Evelyn extended her right hand slowly, shaking her hand gently. She was unsure whether to trust this new person, wondering if this was some kind of good cop/bad cop kind of play in action.

"Honestly Barksley I think you have jumped the gun a bit here. An interview under caution?" Danielle shook her head in disappointment. This was not the first time she had worked a case with DI Barksley and she knew his underhand tactics. "Turn that tape off, there is no need for it."

Barksley took in a long deep breath of annoyance, his intense eyes growing ever more intense, ridges showing on his forehead. Despite the instructions, he left the recording running.

He regained composure before speaking again. "If you would be so kind as to explain yourself Thompson, for the benefit of the recording."

"Certainly sir." Danielle looked over to Barksley, wanting to see the annoyance her news would have on him. "We have started excavating the ground around the body. Initial findings estimate the body to have been in the ground for well over 200 years. The clothing is estimated to be from the late 17th Century. Therefore, there is little need to continue with this interview."

They could all see Barksley was full of rage, his plans for a quick arrest and closing the case before lunch now gone, fearing his record would now be blighted by another potentially unsolved cold case. He banged his clenched fist onto the desk, relieving the tension in his body. He stood up straight and adjusted his jacket.

"Interview terminated at 10:35am." DI Barksley said before pressing a button on the wall of the van, the red light went out, indicating the recording had stopped.

"What the hell is going on?" Evelyn let out her frustration at being accused of potentially murdering her ex-fiance.

DI Barksley was now back in control of his emotions, his calm facade returning. "Earlier today, a Mr Alan Milton was metal detecting on this field. He discovered a wallet and then found a second target further down. He continued digging until he found a ring. The ring was attached to a human skeleton."

"And your first thought was to try and pin a murder on me?" Evelyn said in disgust.

"I am perfectly entitled to make enquiries. You have to admit it is a strange coincidence to find a wallet next to a human skeleton." Barksley commented, trying to justify his dodgy tactics.

David had remained silent throughout this whole ordeal. He thought Barksley had started to respect him and Evelyn after the previous day's events. Now he knew where they really stood.

"So we are free to go." David spoke the statement rather than asking it as a question.

"Yes, get out of my sight!" Barksley growled back at him.

David, Evelyn and Danielle exited the van, Barksley slamming the door behind them. Moments later the sound of DI Barksley shouting into his phone resumed. The three of them walked away from the van to avoid the noise.

Once Evelyn was sure they were out of earshot of the van, she stopped walking and started speaking to Danielle.

"So, now we are no longer suspects, are we able to take a sneak peak at the ring you found?" Evelyn asked Danielle. This was what fascinated David about Evelyn so much. She was able to go from a stressful situation and regain her cool like the flick of a switch. David also knew she was probably pushing her luck here too.

Danielle looked at Evelyn with an eyebrow raised. "You don't waste an opportunity, do you?"

"Well, if you don't ask, you don't get." Evelyn replied.

Danielle paused, mulling it over. She got her phone out of her pocket and unlocked it, about to click on the photos app. Her thumb paused above the touch screen before asking, "What did you say you did for a living again?"

It was questions like this that made David realise how he barely knew his new friend. He hadn't even asked her the question himself before.

"I'm a musician." Evelyn replied.

Danielle nodded, looking assured, she continued speaking whilst opening the photos app and scrolling to the picture she wanted to show. "I was just double checking you weren't a reporter or something. As long as you keep it to yourself you can have a quick look."

Danielle held the phone up so they could both see. The ring, now minus the finger bone, had most of the soil cleaned off and was placed on a white piece of paper with a ruler to help identify the size of the object. The ring appeared to be made of gold, with a large round signet the size of a pound coin. There was a symbol of an animal on the ring. It looked like a mix of a dragon and a lion.

Before they could make out too much detail, Danielle pressed the button on the side of her phone and the screen went blank.

"I heard about your good work yesterday at the church. News travels fast in this job." Danielle smiled a friendly smile before continuing, "That's partly why I wanted to interrupt Barksley whilst he was in full flow of his interrogation, just to take him down a peg or two."

Danielle extended her hand out and shook their hands one after the other.

"Pleasure to be of service, but I have a lot of work to do here so better crack on with it." Danielle said before giving them one last smile and wave over her shoulder whilst walking back towards the white tent, before stopping and turning back. "Musician you say. I'll keep an eye out for your work. Always interested in new music." She carried on walking back to the tent.

David and Evelyn turned in the opposite direction and walked away from the crime scene and back towards Little-Astwick, Evelyn with a big smile on her face.

CHAPTER FOUR

David and Evelyn left the footpath and crossed over the threshold into the village.

"Fancy a cuppa?" David asked.

"Sounds like a great idea." Evelyn replied, before starting to walk over towards the cafe with David following.

David's stomach started growling. "That reminds me, I didn't have time for breakfast today."

Evelyn opened the cafe door and walked in, trying to look casual in front of the good looking Italian owner, Andrea, who was standing at a nearby table taking their order. She smiled and nodded at him politely, but at the first glimpse of her he stopped taking the order, walked over and hugged her, before kissing her on both cheeks in the traditional Italian greeting.

David was halfway through the door taking in the

scene before him, smiling to himself, until Andrea saw him and then rushed over and greeted him in the same manner.

"Ciao! Ciao! So good to see you! Hope you are both ok after last night's events!" Andrea exclaimed.

Evelyn and David, who were not expecting this, both stood there in shock. The events of last night suddenly seemed like a long time ago after the rush of the morning's events so far, but they were surprised the village knew all about it.

Andrea saw the look on their faces and realised he had overstepped. "Forgive me, you have come for a quiet cafe latte and not all this nonsense from me." He gestured to the empty tables in the cafe with his right hand, palm opened. "Please, take a seat and I will be with you shortly."

Andrea returned to the table he was serving and apologised to them before continuing to take their order. David and Evelyn walked past the table and over to a quiet table in the corner, taking their seats. They couldn't hear what Andrea was saying, but they could see table occupants laughing as he laid on his effortless charm. He could make anyone feel welcome, the previous interruption now a distant memory for the people at the table.

"I'm still getting used to the way everyone seems to know everyone's business in a village. It's not like that in the city." David started. He was expecting a witty retort from Evelyn, but she remained quiet. He looked at her, she was still looking at Andrea, a small smile on her face, cheeks glowing red. Andrea turned to walk back to the counter to start making drinks. Evelyn quickly turned away, facing David. He had a childish grin on his face.

"Sorry, you said something about the village?" Evelyn asked, trying to change the subject before David commented about Andrea.

"Yes, I'm still getting used to how fast news travels in a village." David replied.

"And you said something about the city too?" Evelyn asked, suddenly realising she knew barely anything about David's past. Even though she barely knew him, she already knew she could trust him. "Is that where you are from originally?"

"Well, yes." David answered, realising that she was listening even when distracted. "I grew up in the city, living with my Gran in a small apartment."

Evelyn waited for David to continue with his story, but it was clear that was all he wanted to say. She was intrigued now and wanted to delve a little deeper into his back story, unsure whether to leave it be for now or try and gently enquire. She decided to ask about his Gran. That seemed like the polite thing to do.

"So, is your Gran still living in the city or has she moved out to the countryside too?" Evelyn asked.

"Um, well, no, she passed away last year." David began. He looked down at the floor, the story was not one he liked to share. He looked back up to Evelyn and saw her kind and supportive face looking back at him. David thought to himself, maybe it would do him some good to get this out in the open and share it with his new friend. "It's a very sad story really. She was mugged a few years ago whilst walking back from the shops one night. I was working late and wasn't there with her. I normally made sure I was back in time to take her shopping every Thursday, but there was a deadline for some work that had to be done."

David paused and shut his eyes, thinking back to those dark times. "She was never the same after that. She never wanted to go out, she wouldn't even open the curtains for fear of people looking in through the windows. Never answered the door. I tried to get her some help, someone to talk to, but there was no help available. It kept on like this for months, until one morning she just didn't get up. She passed away in her sleep."

Evelyn looked at David, his eyes starting to water, the emotions having risen to the surface.

"It's why I wanted to join the police. I wanted to try and make a difference for someone else so they didn't have to go through that." David finished, tears now running gently down his cheeks.

"I'm so sorry David. I had no idea." Evelyn stood up, walked over to David and gave him a hug. He embraced her back, glad that he had been brave enough to share his story.

"Everything ok?" a questioning voice asked from behind them both.

David and Evelyn stopped hugging and turned around to see Andrea standing behind them, menus in hand.

"I'm sorry if I was a bit much when you came in, it was a natural reaction to seeing you both alive and well. Mi scuso." Andrea apologised, his big brown eyes conveying his sincerity. Evelyn and David both smiled back at him.

"Oh Andre, no it's nothing you have done, we were just talking about something else." Evelyn assured.

Andrea smiled back, happy the others were now smiling back at him. He waited for Evelyn to sit back down before handing them a menu each. "Ok, well here are the menus, can I get you any drinks?"

"Due caffè lattes, per favore!" David answered for them both, whilst also reaching the limit of his knowledge of the Italian language.

"Eccellente." Andrea nodded, appreciating the effort David had made, then walked back to the coffee machine to start making their drinks.

David waited a few seconds, weighing up whether to ask the question on his mind. He decided to try and start the conversation off with a joke to try and lighten the mood. "So is this the first time you have been accused of murder?" David asked with a cheeky smile.

"Well, the first time this week at least…" Evelyn kept an over-serious look on her face for all of three seconds before her laughter broke through.

"In all seriousness, I just wondered how that wallet ended up next to an old skeleton?" David asked.

Evelyn stopped laughing. "I try not to think too much about Steven these days, but I guess I don't really have a choice right now." She closed her eyes and thought for a moment, before opening her eyes and continuing. "I remember buying him a new wallet for his birthday. He lost his old wallet out at the pub one night."

"Ok, do you remember when that was or which pub was it?" David prompted.

"We didn't go out that much back then, saving money for the wedding and our honeymoon." Evelyn paused, shaking her head, now knowing what a waste of time that effort was. "I remember one night we went out. Steven had just got a promotion at work so we went for a meal at the village pub to celebrate. Things should have got a lot easier for us with the pay rise that came with the new job, but well, you know how that ended up."

David nodded in agreement, knowing how Steven walked out on Evelyn a short while later.

"So anything about that night stick out?" David dug a little deeper.

"We both had a lot to drink, well, Steven had a lot more to drink than me, but I still had a few. It was a bit of a blur, getting home and waking up with a headache the next day." Evelyn paused, memories suddenly coming back to her. "In fact, there was someone else there who may remember that night more clearly."

She put her head in her hands to hide her embarrassment. David was waiting for her to continue talking. He wanted to know who they needed to speak to.

Then suddenly he remembered his visit to the pub the previous day and how the man they questioned had known Evelyn from before. He now knew why she was embarrassed.

"George." David said.

Evelyn raised her head out of her hands, took a deep breath and then confirmed the name. "George."

"Well, I don't know about you, but I think we deserve some breakfast to go with our coffees after all the hard work we have done so far today." David said, before taking a look at the menu deciding what to order.

"Yes, I could do with something to get my blood sugar up a bit before speaking to George and going through all that again." Evelyn agreed.

Andrea brought over their cafe lattes and took their food order, David asking Andrea what he would recommend, as everything on the menu sounded great. Andrea simply said, "Leave it to me!" and walked away to start preparing their food.

When he returned with their food, he obviously knew what Evelyn liked based on her previous visits, but he threw in some of his other specialties for David to try. They ate their food and drank their coffee, devouring every morsel, enjoying every mouthful.

Now fully fortified and full of energy, they got up and walked over to the counter to pay. "I hope it was satisfactory?" Andrea asked.

"It was absolutely fantastic!" David replied enthusiastically, getting his wallet out of his pocket ready to hand over his card to pay for the food.

"Hey, it's my turn to pay." Evelyn said, pushing the card back into David's wallet. She retrieved her own card and paid for the meal, before she added. "It's what friends do.".

They smiled at each other, before David shook hands

with Andrea.

Andrea outstretched his right hand to shake Evelyn's hand, but she didn't reciprocate the motion. Andrea suddenly withdrew his hand, a flash of confusion sweeping over his face.

"It's just, well, I think I prefer the Italian greetings over the English." Evelyn said nervously. Andrea smiled, now understanding. He opened his arms up wide and waited for Evelyn to move towards him. They embraced and kissed each other on the cheeks twice whilst saying "Ciao." to each other. Evelyn, now red in the face, walked out quickly out of the cafe. David followed, waving goodbye to Andrea as he walked past the counter and out the front door.

CHAPTER FIVE

The two companions headed towards the village pub to see if George was there. They walked in through the open door, eyes adjusting from the light of the day to the relative darkness of the pub, its walls covered in vintage dark oak panels. The same barmaid as yesterday was cleaning the bar and getting the place ready for the lunchtime patrons.

"You two again. Are you going to buy anything this time?" the barmaid said, looking up from her cleaning work.

"Well, not right now. We were wondering if George was here again?" asked David.

"Not today. Not sure where he is. Probably didn't want to leave home with the police swarming outside his front door." replied the barmaid.

"Outside his front door?" questioned Evelyn.

"Yeah, George lives in the manor house up on Manor farm." The barmaid explained. She carried on cleaning before saying, "If you aren't going to buy a drink then please leave. I've got work to do."

"Just one more question. How long have you worked here?" David asked, wondering if the barmaid might remember a night when George was threatened by Steven Conrad.

The barmaid stopped cleaning again and looked up at them. "I've worked here for a few months. You ordering a drink or what?"

"Ok, never mind. We will get out of your way." said David, holding up his hands apologetically.

David and Evelyn looked at each other, eyebrows raised, before walking out of the pub and into the daylight.

"Well that's that then," said David. "I think we should stay clear of the manor house for a bit. We don't want to antagonise Barksley any more if we can avoid it."

"Come on David, where's your sense of adventure gone?" Evelyn said.

This time David had an answer for her. "I didn't say we were done. Let's put the wallet enquiries on hold for now. How about we go and visit Alan and get a bit more information about what he saw?"

"Ooh, yes. Now that's the spirit." Evelyn replied, nodding gently in agreement.

Alan Milton lived a couple of streets away from the pub. They walked down the hill towards the church and then took a right to get to his house. David knocked on the wooden door of the cottage. It had stone walls, small glass leaded windows, and a tile roof with a chimney poking out the top on one side. Well established ivy was growing up the walls of the building, finishing off the classic country cottage look. Next to the house was a free standing garage, the wooden doors wide open, but no car inside, just an oil stain on the floor.

They waited for a minute or so before the door opened a crack and a slither of a face appeared in the gap. The door was on a chain, preventing somebody from forcing the door fully open.

"Yes?" the slither of face asked.

"Good morning. My name is David Morgan, I'm a community support officer, and this is my friend Evelyn..." David started before he was broken off.

"Evelyn McKenzie? Like the name in the wallet?" the slither of face asked, tension in his voice, his eyes growing wider with fear.

"Yes, that is correct Mr Milton. It is Mr Alan Milton, isn't it? We just wanted to ask you some questions about this morning's events." David spoke in his quiet and docile tones. He remembered his Gran and the shock that events could have on people. He wanted to try and calm down the situation so he added, "We can come back later if needed.".

The face at the door seemed calmer, weighing up what to say, before adding "Ah, no, it's fine."

The door shut slightly as the chain was removed, before the door swung open fully. They were still unable to enter as Alan stood in the doorway holding the door open, still in a state of shock.

"May we come in?" Evelyn asked.

Alan looked them both up and down for a few seconds, before agreeing. "Oh, yes, of course.", before he let go of the door and walked into the house, sitting down in his living room. David and Evelyn followed, shutting the door behind them, before following Alan into his living room and sitting in chairs facing Alan's armchair.

"I told people on the phone what I know, when I called the police. I found the wallet, then the ring, then the...", he blurted out, before suddenly pausing, not wanting to say finger, "the bone."

David thought back over his training. He needed to get Alan to calm down, change the subject, maybe make some small talk. He was considering his options of how to continue, but someone got there first.

"Metal detecting seems like fun. Have you done it for long?" Evelyn asked. Alan looked over to Evelyn. He thought back to when he found the wallet and saw her name on the card. He imagined that the body could have belonged to either of the names in the wallet. Now he knew that he could rule out one of the names.

Alan loved metal detecting. He could, and quite often did, talk about it for hours. Alan now smiled a small smile, the edges of his lips turning slightly upward. "Yes, it is my passion. Walking fields with the steady beep, beep, beep in your ear, waiting for the excitement of a find, waiting for the beeps to get closer together, finding something that has been lost to the world for many years."

He stood up and walked over to a wooden framed cabinet at the side of the living room. It had two tall glass doors that allowed you to see row upon row of shelves with various finds in different conditions. On the top of the cabinet was a framed piece of paper. One that David and Evelyn recognised instantly as the family tree of the Templeton family, an exact copy of the one hanging in Michelle's hallway.

Alan put his hand in his right trouser pocket and pulled out a small key, using it to unlock the glass doors. He opened the doors and plucked something off the middle of a shelf towards the top. He returned to his chair, sat down and then outstretched his palm, a small shiny object within his hand.

"Here we have a rather unusual object. A gold coin." he paused whilst the two in front of him sat forward in their chairs to get a better look, just as they always did whenever he showed people. There was something about gold that always interested people. "It's from the late 17th century, William of Orange."

"Oh wow, can I take a closer look?" Evelyn asked.

"No." came the abrupt reply from Alan. "It's very precious to me I'm afraid."

"Oh, how so?" Evelyn asked.

Alan knew how to get people interested. Hook them and reel them in with his story that he had told a hundred times before, perfecting it a little more each time. "You see, I found this coin whilst searching for a legend. A tale that goes back centuries. A story of trust and betrayal."

Alan stood and quietly cleared his throat, ensuring the story he was about to tell had its maximum impact.

"A local family once lived in an estate not too far from here. They could trace their roots almost back to William the Conqueror, a stones-throw from royalty, such was their grandeur. They were an important family, regularly attending the courts of kings and queens of England, retiring to their country estate not far from where we now stand. They had a modest country house, until the late 17th century when they faced the devastation of a fire."

"Instead of remaining in despair, they used this situation to their advantage, improving upon their old home and building a much grander house, a reflection of the family's stature. The house was completed and they then turned their attention to the estate grounds. They wanted to build a wonder of the age, a garden fit for the monarch that was planning on visiting them at their country house the next summer. Such occurrences were few and far between."

"But not all went as planned. The work started but never finished. They were betrayed by their architect. The architect of their demise." Alan paused for dramatic effect, waiting for the perfect moment to reach the climax of his story.

Unfortunately this particular audience didn't play along.

"Arthur Androse?" said Evelyn at the same time as Alan said the name.

Alan looked down his nose at Evelyn. "Yes, Arthur Androse." He puffed in disappointment at his wasted storytelling skills. He flexed the fingers of his free hand by his side open and closed as a coping mechanism.

"We only found out about this story ourselves yesterday." David chimed in. "So what's the coin got to do with Arthur Androse?"

Alan looked down to the small gold coin in his hand, taking in its magnificence. David could see the gold reflecting in Alan's eyes.

"This is but one piece of the fee paid to Arthur Androse by the Templeton family. The rest has been lost to time. No one knows its whereabouts. This piece was found in the local school grounds. A full search was made of the area but none others were found, just this single piece of brilliant gold."

"That's a fascinating story. Now, can we go back to this morning?" David asked.

Alan sat back down, David noted his mood now resembled pure boredom. At least it was better than the state of shock they found him in.

"Yes, like I said, I found the wallet before I found the ring." Alan replied, a look of disappointment flashed over his face as he said the word 'ring'.

"Ok, but can we go back a step further, why were you metal detecting in that field? Was there a find there previously?" David enquired.

"I was asked to… I mean," he paused, thinking before continuing, "it was my idea to investigate around the village. We are lucky to live in a village full of history. We are learning things all the time that have been lost to time."

"Yes, like Androse's gold?" Evelyn suggested.

"Yes…" Alan answered instinctively, before continuing, "but today's search had nothing to do with that. It was mere speculation on my part."

"Ok, is there anything else you can tell us about today?" David asked.

"I'd rather not think about it too much to be honest. The image of that finger in my hand keeps repeating in my mind." Alan said.

Evelyn had sat patiently whilst Alan had given his story and David had asked his questions. She had one more thing she wanted to ask Alan.

"The ring you found, do you recall if there were any symbols on it?" Evelyn asked.

"There was something on it, but I can't recall what it was. Maybe an animal or something?" Alan answered vaguely. Evelyn frowned for a second, Alan's answer not sitting right with her.

"Ok, thanks. We had better be on our way to rejoin our colleagues near the manor house." Evelyn smiled and stood up to leave.

"Oh well if you are heading back to the manor house, there is a shortcut at the end of this street that will take you there. Quicker than walking back past the pub." Alan informed them.

"Well, that's great to know. I think that is everything we need to know. Thank you again for your time." David stood, ready to leave, but he was interrupted by Alan holding out his free hand without the coin to block his way.

"I recognise your names now. You were the two involved in the church last night?" Alan questioned, but already sure of the answer.

"Yes, that was us. News does travel fast." David joked.

"Yes, indeed." Alan laughed, before turning suddenly serious. "And what did you find down there? Under the church?"

David was taken aback, unsure how to answer. Luckily he wasn't alone.

"I'm sure David would love to tell you all the details at a later date, but it's part of an ongoing investigation." Evelyn answered for him.

"Yes, sorry." David smiled and nodded in agreement.

"You found something down there didn't you?" Alan moved closer, looking David in the eye, getting more intense by the moment.

David did not like how this was going and thought to himself it was time to leave.

"Thank you for all your assistance today Mr Milton."

David spoke, whilst pushing Alan's arm down gently. "I'm sure we will be in touch again in the near future."

David and Evelyn walked towards the front door and opened it, whilst Alan stood still watching them suspiciously. They walked out the door and started closing it. Only then did Alan move, but towards his glass cabinet rather than the front door.

They shut the door and walked away from the house. By instinct they started walking the way they came, but then Evelyn stopped and looked in the opposite direction. Looking for the path that Alan had mentioned. She had lived in the village for a few years but never known about another path to the manor house.

David noticed she had stopped walking and turned and retraced his steps towards her.

"You ok?" David asked.

"Yeah, well no, not really." Evelyn replied, then asked, "Alan creeped you out right? It wasn't just me?"

"Yes definitely creeped me out too." David agreed. "He's definitely hiding something, but at the same time I think he is trying to tell us something. I don't think I've met anyone quite like him before."

"Hmm." replied Evelyn, for once not sure what to say.

"So are we going this way now then?" David asked.

"Oh, yes." Evelyn seemed to wake from her thoughts, "Alan mentioned the other path. I don't think I've been this way before. Let's try it out."

"Ok, let's go." David agreed, they both started walking towards the end of the road looking for a path. They reached the end of the road and looked from left to right.

"There it is!" Evelyn said, pointing to her right. The path was hidden from view unless you were right at the end of the street. A strange optical illusion of hedges overlapping prevented you seeing it from other directions. There were also no signs for the footpath either.

David got his phone out of his pocket and opened his mapping app and zoomed into his current location. He couldn't see the path on his map either?

"It's not signposted and it's not on my map, but it heads in the right direction." David said, unsure.

"Nothing ventured, nothing gained." replied Evelyn. They nodded in agreement and started walking down the path.

CHAPTER SIX

They followed the path for a few hundred metres before it started heading gently downhill. The path was flagged by trees on either side, the branches reaching high overhead and intertwining with one another, creating a tunnel-like effect high up over the top of the path.

The branches combined to block out most of the sunlight, preventing any large plants from growing along the floor. Small patches of sunlight lit the way ahead as the tree branches moved slightly side to side in the gentle breeze revealing small gaps for the light to break through.

Eventually, the path headed slowly back uphill, still surrounded by the tunnel-like tree cover with a small gap in the hedge ahead now visible. They headed towards it, wondering where it would emerge.

The tree coverage grew a bit thinner, allowing them

to see through the small holes into the fields either side. To their left was a field with golden crops growing, swaying gently in the light breeze. To their right was the field with police vans, cars and the tent.

They emerged out of the gap in the hedge and onto a small lane, the manor house just over to their right. David looked back over to where they had just come from. He could barely see where they had just emerged.

"Well, here we are!" said David.

"And we managed to avoid Barksley too!" said Evelyn.

"Let's go see if George is in, shall we?" David smiled in anticipation.

"If we must." replied Evelyn with a look of trepidation on her face.

They walked over to the manor house, opened the metal gate and started walking down the well worn garden path. There was a very tidy grass lawn on either side of the walkway, with flower beds either side of the entrance. The grand, red painted, oak front door was directly in front of them, but they took the opportunity to take in the features of the old building as they moved closer. The walls were built from thick brown ironstone blocks with the windows edged in a lighter creamy cotswold stone, creating a beautiful contrast between the two different materials. The building had large sash windows showing the high ceilings of the rooms inside. The oak front door had a large imposing granite lintel above it with a circle engraved into it, looking strangely weathered and worn compared to the rest of the polished granite.

David raised his hand to knock politely, but he was beaten to it by Evelyn thumping her hand on the door, shouting "Police, open up!". The both smiled at each other, acknowledging their own private joke. They hoped someone answered as they had little hope of getting through a solid wood door that thick.

After about thirty seconds a loud clunking noise emerged from the old fashioned lock, before the door slowly creaked open on its antique hinges. In the doorway stood George, his frame almost filling the whole doorway, dressed in dark blue denim jeans and a crisply ironed shirt, in wide contrast to his mass of unkempt dark hair.

"Hello again!" George exclaimed as he lurched forward and grabbed them both, one in each arm, lifting them slightly off the ground so they had to go on tip toes as he embraced them. "Thank you for saving Jez!"

David tried to answer, but realised he could barely breathe whilst in George's grip. Evelyn must have had a bit more room as she was able to reply.

"Anytime George, glad to be of service" Evelyn said in a slightly higher pitch than normal. "Any chance you could let us go now?"

"Oh, yeah, of course." George said, lowering them gently back to their feet as he released them from his powerful arms. He walked back into the house, beckoning them in with his right hand waving. "Come on in!"

David and Evelyn took a second to regain their breath before following George shutting the door behind them, the hinges complaining once more with a creak. The modest hallway led them into a large square room with a wide, burgundy red carpeted staircase that started on the left of the wall directly in front of them, before turning the corner and following the next wall as they rose to the next floor up. Each wall had a doorway leading deeper into the house. The floor of the room was lined with large dark stone tiles. There were a few paintings on the walls showing the previous residents of the house in their Georgian or Victorian outfits.

George walked through a door on their left which led them into the living room with a large fireplace and three antique sofas. There were another two doorways, one leading through to what looked like a dining room, whilst the other some kind of study with books along the walls. The floor was also tiled with large flat stones, but this room also had a large rug in the centre for a bit more comfort.

They all sat down on the sofas to talk.

"I've just got back from the hospital, went to see Jez this morning. That's why I've got my good shirt on for a change." George began. "His head is still a bit fuzzy, doctors say it will take a few days but he should be back to normal. He said to pass on his thanks to his saviours. I assume he was talking about you two rather than God this time, but you can never be sure with a vicar."

"That's great news. He was in a bit of a state when we found him last night." replied Evelyn.

"That reminds me, there was a police guard at the door of the next room. I can only assume it was for Michelle. But I didn't bother visiting her." George commented. "Imagine having them so close after what she did to him!"

David had tried to keep thoughts of Michelle out of his head after facing the threat of a kitchen knife. It was comforting knowing that she was under police guard.

"I know, but let's focus on the good news about Gerome and not worry about Michelle. She will get her just deserts in prison." Evelyn reassured George.

"This house is pretty amazing!" said David, trying to change the subject.

"Yeah, it ain't bad. Bit draughty in the winter but

a good excuse to light a big fire in the fireplace." George pointed to the grand fireplace as he spoke. The fire was unlit today, but it was all built up ready to go when needed, with additional dried wood stored in a basket nearby.

"Is it just you living here?" David asked.

"Yeah, just me. I was an only child and my parents have passed on now." George looked down at the floor for a moment remembering them, before he looked back up and joked, "I'm still waiting to meet Mrs right.", lightening the mood once more, David and Evelyn chuckling along with George.

David looked over to Evelyn wondering if she was going to start the questioning or whether he had to initiate it. She took a deep breath and then nodded in understanding.

"So did you see all the police in the field opposite?" Evelyn asked George.

"Yeah, I could hardly miss it, could I! Saw them all as I got back from the hospital." George said. "Thought I'd done and got myself into trouble again last night, but I had a quiet one without Jez to talk to."

"Speaking of getting into trouble…" Evelyn began with a smile, "You remember the chat we had yesterday, when we talked about my ex trying to start a fight with you?"

"Oh yeah, then you sticking your tongue down his

throat to stop him?" George asked.

"Yeah, um, that's it." Evelyn said, going red in the face with embarrassment once more. "Well, from what I remembered, we left and headed home, but couldn't find Steven's wallet the next day. Do you know what happened to it?"

George's smile disappeared, his cheeks turning slightly more pink with embarrassment of his own.

"Well, yes, sorry about that." began George, looking sheepish. "I saw you go and leave the wallet on the table. I grabbed it and headed outside to give it back to you, or maybe throw it at him, I hadn't decided yet. But then I saw you too embracing down the road under the moonlight and instead of being angry, I realised I felt jealous of you two."

Evelyn looked into George's big eyes trying to comfort him.

"So, I decided to keep it and headed home instead. You know, out of spite." George looked apologetically back at Evelyn, hoping she would understand. "I got home, grabbed a shovel and dug a small hole and buried the bloody thing in the field. Completely forgot about it until you reminded me to be fair. Sorry."

Evelyn smiled back at George, showing no hard feelings between them.

"Honestly, it doesn't matter. We just wanted to know

how it got in the field." Evelyn explained.

George turned to David, his face suddenly twisted into confusion. "But why are all these police here for a missing wallet?"

"Oh, well, it's actually a bit more than that." David explained. "A body was also found near the wallet."

"A body!" George stood up, shocked. "Out there, just a stone's throw from my house!"

George hurried over to the window to take a look at the activity with renewed interest, his large hands on the back of his head, flattening down his hair.

"They said it's been there for well over two hundred years." Evelyn said, trying to calm George down. It seemed to have some effect on George, his hands came down to his side and his breathing slowed down a bit.

"It couldn't be, could it?" George muttered quietly to himself.

George turned to Evelyn and took her arms gently in his large hands. He crouched down slightly so he could look into Evelyn's eyes better as he spoke calmly. "Please, tell me everything you know."

Evelyn looked back into George's large brown eyes, somehow feeling calm and reassured by George's gentle grip. "Alan was doing some metal detecting this morning in the field, when he found the wallet. He then found another hit further down and discovered the bones. I got put in the frame for murder by DI Barksley, before a forensic scientist interrupted the interrogation to tell us the bones had been there a long time. We went to see Alan to talk to him about the wallet, which brought us here. There isn't much more to tell."

George was obviously hoping for more, his head started drooping down in disappointment. The room filled with silence for a few moments before David chipped in.

"Well, and the ring too." David added quietly.

George's head shot back up, eyes looking back at Evelyn.

"Oh yes, the ring." Evelyn said. "Alan discovered a ring on the finger. A large gold signet ring with some kind of crest on it. Some kind of animal, maybe a dragon or lion."

"Do you have a picture of it?" George asked, speaking hurriedly.

"No, but the forensic scientist showed us a picture. We could try and ask her again for it." Evelyn replied.

"Officer Thompson," David replied.

"Sorry?" George asked.

"Officer Thompson." David repeated. "She was the

forensic scientist that showed us the ring."

George carefully let go of Evelyn's arms and stood back up straight, before turning to look out the window once more. He stood still for about 30 seconds muttering something inaudible to the others. He stopped talking and suddenly turned around and smiled a forced smile.

"Well, thank you for coming over, but I've actually got some business to attend to so if you could see yourselves out that would be great." George said, before turning and heading for the adjacent room filled with books, shutting the door behind him.

David and Evelyn looked at each other wondering what that was all about. They stood up and walked out the house, opening and closing the creaky old wooden door behind them.

Before they could start talking about what to do next David's phone started pinging. He retrieved his phone from his pocket and unlocked the screen, checking his notifications.

"What the…?" David said, a look of grave concern on his face.

CHAPTER SEVEN

"Well, what is it!" Evelyn asked David. He had been standing watching something on his phone for over a minute without saying anything. The look of concern turned into confusion.

"David!" Evelyn shouted this time, finally breaking David's daze.

"My house has been broken into!" David muttered in disbelief. He showed his phone to Evelyn, pressing play on the video he had just watched. It started off with a black and white view of a small garden, a grass lawn surrounded by dark wooden fences on the left and right and a hedge to the rear. Something appeared in the top left of the video, a long thin shape flickering in and out of the view quickly before it stopped moving completely. Evelyn moved her face closer to the screen to try and see in more detail. Another long thin shape appeared next to the original shape, remaining still once more. The stationary shapes moved again, before it flashed across the screen covering the centre of the video, revealing the object to be legs belonging to a large spider.

"Ah!" gasped Evelyn in horror, moving her face away from the phone. "What did you show me that for?"

David looked at the screen. "Oops, sorry, wrong video." replied David sheepishly. He pressed the screen a couple of times, then held the phone out for Evelyn to watch once more. She looked at him angrily for a few seconds before focusing intently on the phone screen once more.

The same view of the garden appeared, but this time there was movement by the hedge at the back of the garden. Evelyn moved a little closer to see what was happening. A gloved hand appeared, followed by an arm, then a leg before the full body dressed in black emerged from the thick hedge, the face covered by a balaclava. Once free of the hedge, the person headed quickly towards the camera and pulled out what appeared to be a strange shaped knife from their pocket, the handle having a slight kink before the serrated blade started. The unknown person wedged it between the window frame, leveraging the blade upwards, forcing the lock on the sash window to snap. They put the knife back in their pocket and opened the window, entering the building.

Without further movement, the video went blank, before starting once more triggered by the character emerging from the window and running back to the hedge, forcing their way through the thick foliage before disappearing completely. The video went blank once more with no more movement to trigger the motion activated camera.

"What did I just watch?" Evelyn asked, confused.

"That was from the remote camera on my house." David replied, his face pale with shock. "Someone just broke into my house!"

"What!" Evelyn responded in amazement. "Quick, we've got to get there and see what's happened!"

David looked around him, suddenly remembering he had no transport. They had walked here, but where was his bike? It suddenly dawned on him that he had left his bike leaning against the police van in the field opposite the house. He had been so shocked by the interrogation tactics of DI Barksley earlier that he had left his bike unattended in the field. The field, full of police.

David ran towards a gate that led into the field, swinging it open, running through with no thought of closing it, before ducking under the police tape and making a beeline for the largest police van. He knocked furiously on the door of the van, hoping that DI Barksley was still there.

"Yes." came the reply from the van. David opened the door and saw DI Barksley sat at a small desk, reading from a file.

"Barksley, I need your help! Right now!" David shouted, panicked.

Barksley put the folder down, sighed, took a deep breath, then stood up, walking over to the door where David was. "Let's start again shall we. What appears to be the issue?"

"I just saw a video, someone's broken..." David started.

"What is my name?" Barksley interrupted.

David stopped talking. He didn't have time for this protocol bullshit, but he realised he had no choice but to play along with his game. David took a deep breath before speaking again, regaining control. "Detective Inspector Barksley." he said calmly.

"Yes, hello Mr Morgan. How may I be of assistance?" Barksley said back in his condescending tone.

"There has been a break in at my house. I have a video. I kindly request permission to take one of these police vehicles to go and investigate." David answered, equally as condescending as Barkley's tone. He held the video up so Barksley could see the person entering the house.

"Ah you see, that wasn't so difficult was it..." Barksley began, before stopping and taking in what David had just said coupled with the video footage.

He followed up with a simple response. "Follow me."

Barksley exited the van and walked over towards a police car at the edge of the field, with David following. Evelyn had caught up by this point and was following them both towards the car. Once they reached it, they could see Officer Smith sitting in the driver's seat, taking a sip of coffee from his thermos mug.

"Officer Smith, I am sequestering this vehicle." Barksley stated authoritatively.

Officer Smith gulped down the mouthful of hot coffee and looked at DI Barksley through the window in bewilderment.

"OUT... NOW!" Barksley shouted at Officer Smith. This time he got the message. Opening the door and exiting the vehicle as quickly as he could. In his rush, the thermos mug slipped from his hand, landing in a large patch of mud, coffee slowly dripping out of the now filthy mouthpiece.

David got in the passenger seat, with Evelyn getting in the back of the car. They were still mid way through putting their seatbelts on when Barksley started the engine and gunned it out of the field and onto the small lane, lights and sirens blaring to warn any nearby traffic of the fast moving vehicle.

Officer Smith bent down and picked up his coffee cup to prevent it spilling its entire contents, then tried to wipe the dirt off with his sleeve. He took a small sip, before immediately spitting it back out again, the remaining coffee tainted by the soil.

In the passenger seat of the fast moving car, David hung on to the door handle to help brace himself against the rapid changes of direction, before informing Barksley of his address. Barksley simply replied "Affirmative.", nodding to confirm his understanding. Evelyn's eyes were wide, taking in her surroundings at a speed she had never had to experience before.

Three minutes later they pulled up outside the house, screeching to a halt. David and Barksley jumped out of the front seats, with Barksley pausing a moment to release the rear door so that Evelyn could get out from the back seat.

They raced along the short gravel path to the front door of the house, seeing the blue wooden front door still shut as David had left it this morning. He retrieved his key and inserted it into the lock, but before he could turn it, Barksley put his hand over the top of David's, stopping him from opening the door.

"I will go in first and assess the situation, with you behind me." Barksley whispered in an authoritative tone. He then turned to Evelyn and spoke again. "Stay outside until we determine it is safe. Touch nothing as there may be forensic evidence.".

Evelyn nodded silently in agreement. With the

instructions dealt and agreed, Barksley removed his hand and let David unlock the door. He pushed the door slightly ajar, listening for any sounds of movement from within. He pushed the door fully open then took a small, cautious step inside, taking in his surroundings.

"This is the police!" Barksley shouted at no one in particular, making their presence known to anyone lingering inside.

The house was a small two-up two-down arrangement, the front door leading directly into the living room with the stairs directly in front of him on his left hand side. Beyond the stairs was a door leading through to a small kitchen/dining room. The living room had plain white washed walls with no pictures, an old and worn, but clean, light grey carpet on the floor. In the right hand corner was a small desk, with the TV in the centre of the room and a small sofa opposite, under the window.

The outside of the house was how David had left it, but the inside was not. Where there was once order, it had now been replaced with chaos. The papers that had been neatly filed away in the drawers of the desk were now strewn across the floor, the laptop that had been positioned at just the right angle on the desk was now lying on its side, the screen smashed.

Barksley stepped around as much of the paper as he could, making his way towards the kitchen/dining room. He paused before walking over the threshold, listening intently once more for any noise that would give away a waiting attacker. After a few moments he was obviously sure there were none, so he stepped through to the kitchen and looked around.

On his left hand side was a small galley style kitchen with only a few cupboards, with the essential fittings of a kitchen sink and tap and the cooker, fridge and washing machine. The other side of the room had a small table and chairs for four people to sit. There were a couple of boxes in the far right hand corner that had been tipped over, spilling their contents onto the floor, probably from the attacker entering and exiting the room via the open window which was directly above the boxes. Pieces of the broken window lock were scattered over the floor. Next to the window was an external door that led out to the small garden, still shut firm with no signs of attempted entry.

Barksley looked out of the window, taking in the garden and the hedge at the back. He then turned to David suggesting they took a look upstairs. Barksley went first, with David following again. They checked the bathroom and the two bedrooms, one completely empty, the other containing David's bed and wardrobe, but everything was left as it was when he left.

They walked back downstairs and Barksley poked

his head out the front door to speak to Evelyn. She had waited outside as instructed, but had also had a quick peek through the front window to see what had been going on, her curiosity getting the better of her.

"It's ok to come in now we have cleared the building." Barksley told Evelyn, before he walked back into the living room. David stood, looking at the mess, trying to make sense of it all.

Barksley stood with his arms crossed, looking at David and Evelyn, before speaking. "Right then you two. What are your thoughts?".

Evelyn thought about making a snide remark about how Barksley was the detective in the room, but decided against it. Maybe he was testing them, giving them a chance to show their skills.

David retrieved his notebook from his pocket and opened it to a new page. He began writing at the same time as he spoke, taking pauses at the end of each sentence to give him time to catch up his writing with his talking. "At 12:35pm, according to the timestamp on the video, an assailant entered the house through the rear window after forcing it open. They then proceeded to the living room and emptied the drawers of the desk before smashing the laptop computer. The upstairs rooms seem untouched. The assailant then left the house via the same window they entered at 12:39pm."

Barksley nodded, then turned to Evelyn to see what she spotted.

"Well, they were obviously looking for something, maybe something small enough to fit in the desk drawers. We don't know if they found what they were looking for or whether they gave up and ran off." Evelyn commented. David continued writing down Evelyn's observations into his notebook. She looked around the room one more time. "One thing I'm not sure about is why smash the laptop? If they were looking for something physical then why smash the laptop too?"

"I think I know why." David had a sudden thought. "The camera system that sent the footage to my mobile phone is also hooked up to the laptop. It triggers an alert and plays the video on the laptop too. Maybe they saw it and thought they would destroy the evidence by smashing the laptop."

"That's something to go on at least." Barksley nodded a small nod of his head. He was impressed but didn't want to admit it to them. "I'll radio this into HQ and get a team over to see if we can get any forensic evidence."

He went to walk out the front door. He paused and turned back to face David and said, "By the way, what do you think they were looking for?"

David racked his brains, "There was nothing in the drawers apart from some bills and paperwork for the house. I've only been here a couple of weeks and don't really have much here. The only thing worth anything was the computer and now that's been destroyed."

DI Barksley looked David in the eye, weighing up what he saw in someone when questioning them. He must have decided that he believed what David had told him, as he turned and walked back outside, taking his phone out of his pocket to call the station.

David and Evelyn were now alone in the house. Evelyn grabbed David's arm, pulling him gently into the kitchen and further away from Barksley.

"Remember why you called me this morning?" Evelyn whispered to David.

David looked at her, thinking. His mind was obviously still in a state of shock from having his house broken into, but Evelyn was thinking clearly. He retraced the morning in his mind. He had called her to meet him and go to the Manor house to speak to Barksley, but before that he had called her about the leather cylinder! He instinctively moved his hand down to his right jacket pocket, feeling the cylinder through the material of the jacket. He breathed a sigh of relief knowing it was still safe.

"You think this is all because of what we found in the church yesterday?" David whispered back to Evelyn. He went to undo the zip pocket and retrieve the cylinder, but Evelyn put her hand over his and stopped him.

"Not here, we don't know if we can trust Barksley." Evelyn nodded her head to the side in the general direction of the front door a few metres away.

"You don't think he would have anything to do with this, do you?" David asked in surprise.

"I don't know what to think, but all I do know is that we should keep this between us for now." Evelyn finished, David nodding in agreement.

Evelyn started walking back into the living room, whilst David took another quick look at his kitchen. Something about the boxes caught his eye. He walked closer to the box that had been on top and noticed a small black mark on it. He was sure the mark hadn't been there before. He wrote down his observation in his notebook, before placing it and the pen back into his jacket pocket.

He stood up and followed Evelyn out of the kitchen. She was now on her way out the front door so David followed too. Barksley was finishing up his phone conversation and hung up as they emerged from the house.

"Forensics will be here shortly, in the meantime I have ordered Officer Smith to get himself here to wait for their arrival." Barksley smiled at David. "Hope you don't mind but I suggested he sequestered your bicycle."

David and Evelyn smiled back.

"When Smith gets here I suggest you go and speak to your neighbours and take some statements." Barksley said. David and Evelyn understood it was an order rather than a suggestion. "I am needed back at the Manor, there has been a development. You will have to arrange alternative transport back to Little-Astwick."

With that, he walked back down the garden path and got into the waiting police car. He disappeared in the same way that he arrived, much too fast and with the lights flashing and sirens blaring.

David went back inside and retrieved a spare house key for Officer Smith whilst they waited for him to arrive. The key was on a hook at the bottom of the stairs, next to where his jacket had been hanging that morning. He was reassured that the key was still there and had not been taken. He looked around at the mess, fighting the urge to tidy it up, knowing that he had to wait for forensics to do their job. He shook his head at the turn of events and headed back outside.

Officer Smith took a lot longer to arrive than they had thought, arriving on David's bike. David had managed the journey in less than fifteen minutes earlier that morning, but Officer Smith took forty. Smith retrieved his thermos mug, now nice and clean, from the bottle holder of the bike, before he deliberately dropped the bike onto the floor, causing some minor scratches.

"Oops, my mistake." Officer Smith said sarcastically, before walking over to the open front door, leaving the bike in the middle of the road. He took up position at the front door, looked down his nose at David and Evelyn, then took a swig of coffee from his thermos mug. "Hope you don't mind, but I told Andy, or whatever his name is at the coffee shop, to put a coffee on your tab for me."

David walked over to his bike and picked it up. He wheeled the bike over to a small bike shed in his front garden, unlocked the shed, put away the bike and then locked the shed once more.

Smith took another sip of his coffee, then looked back at David and Evelyn with a smug look on his face. "You already know what I'm going to say."

"Shoo?" suggested Evelyn sarcastically.

"Correct," said Officer Smith, using his free hand to make a shooing motion in their direction.

David and Evelyn rolled their eyes in sync with each other before walking out the garden and heading to the closest neighbours house.

CHAPTER EIGHT

David's nearest neighbours, a Mr and Mrs Daniels, hadn't seen or heard anything. David wasn't surprised as he could barely hear them talk over the sound of the television. It was a similar story across the road at Mrs Rones house, she was hoovering the stairs at the time of the incident. David and Evelyn worked their way around the block until they got to the last house on the street.

They approached the black metal gate that led to the house and immediately noticed the sign that read 'Beware of the dog!'. David opened the gate with caution, looking from left to right across the grass for any sign of a dog. Evelyn made sure to shut the gate firmly behind them to prevent any dogs from escaping.

David retrieved his notebook from his jacket pocket, whilst Evelyn knocked on the door. Immediately a dog started barking loudly from inside the house. A few moments later they heard a lady shouting from inside the house, at what they could only assume was aimed at the dog. "It's okay sweetie, my poor darling.", at which point the dog stopped barking and the door was opened a few seconds later.

"Hello there. Can I help you?" the lady replied. She was tall and thin, with dark hair, greying around the roots and temples. She wore a smart designer trouser suit.

"Hello there, my name is David Morgan, a police community support officer, and this is Evelyn." David said, introducing themselves to the resident. "Do you mind me asking what your name is?"

"Oh but of course, my name is Enid." the lady replied.

"Hello Enid." David wrote the house number and the residents name down in his notebook before continuing, "We won't take much of your time, but wanted to inform you there was a break in at a house down the street earlier today, around 12:30 pm, and wondered if you saw or heard anything unusual?"

"Well, let me think." Enid said as she retrieved her phone from her pocket. "Ah yes, from 11:30 to 1 I was on a video conference call, then at 1 I started my lunch meeting."

"Ok, so did you notice anything unusual during your call?" Evelyn asked. The dog started barking once more, from somewhere within the house.

"Oh precious, no need to worry. These are friendly people." Enid shouted back towards the house. The dog went quiet after hearing her owner's voice.

"Precious? Is that the name of your dog?" David asked.

"Heavens no, she's called Sparkles." replied Enid, matter of factly. "Actually, Sparkles has just reminded me of something. There was a loud bang around 12:40. Sparkles was besides herself. I had to pause my video call and comfort her for a good five minutes before I could rejoin."

"I know the feeling. My dog Charlie sometimes goes a bit crazy when a loud motorbike drives through our village." Evelyn contributed.

"Ok, and what did the noise sound like to you?" David asked, trying to gain a bit more insight.

"Well, I had my headset on for the video call so one ear was covered and I was listening intently to my clients discussing their affairs, so I didn't hear it that well. Sometimes the video quality isn't great, the downside to living in a lovely village in the English countryside." Enid replied.

"Affairs, so are you a marriage counsellor then?" Evelyn asked.

"Oh heavens no dear." Enid laughed. "Sorry to disappoint you but I'm a business consultant, it's just the jargon that comes with the job I'm afraid."

"Ok so to go back to the sound, can you describe it?" David asked again, trying to get back onto the subject at hand.

"Tell you what, I can do even better than that. I record all my video calls. Give me five minutes and I will send you a snippet of the call. I can't give you the whole call without you signing a ream of non disclosure agreements." Enid walked back into her house, leaving the door open.

She reappeared a few minutes later holding her phone.

"Can you turn on your NFC?" Enid asked them both.

"Sorry, what?" David replied.

"Pass me your phone please." Enid replied, her hand outstretched waiting for David to hand her his phone. She tapped the back of the phones together, a pinging noise emitting from the phones, followed by another pinging noise to indicate the transfer had finished. She handed the phone back to David. "There, all done. It will be in your photos app."

David opened his photos app as instructed and saw the five second video. He turned the volume up and pressed play.

"I want to touch base on... BANG!", the video played then immediately followed by Sparkles barking madly.

"So a short sharp bang, like a gunshot?" guessed Evelyn.

"Let's not jump to conclusions Evelyn." David said, not wanting to start rumours in the village. "Thank you so much Enid, you have been extremely useful. If you think of anything else, then please give me a call."

David reached for a card from his pocket to leave with Enid, but she put her hand up politely to stop him. "There is no need for that my dear. I synced you as a contact when I transferred the video to you using NFC."

David paused for a moment, no idea what Enid had just said to him, so he removed his hand from his pocket without retrieving a card and smiled back at Enid.

"That's great. Thanks." he eventually said, putting away his notebook back into his pocket. Trying to think of a way to end the conversation on a positive friendly note, he added, "Maybe Sparkles and Charlie could have a playdate at some point."

"I'm sure that would be lovely." Enid replied. "Have a wonderful day."

David and Evelyn waved and walked out the garden as Enid shut the door, a new wave of barking started from Sparkles the dog at the noise of the door shutting.

David walked out of the garden gate with Evelyn following her. Instead of turning back towards David's house, he walked around the house and looked behind it. There was a small single track lane, which he started walking down.

"Where are we going?" Evelny asked, as she followed behind David.

"I didn't think of this before, but there is a little lane here that runs at the back of these houses, and behind my house." David explained.

They walked in silence, David preoccupied with looking over the tall hedge that ran along the side of the lane facing the houses. He was looking at the roofs of the houses, trying to determine which one was his.

"Ah, here we go," David exclaimed. He could see through his upstairs window into his room from here but not much else. He stepped back from the hedge and stood at the other side of the narrow lane, taking in the scene in front of him.

"Look, you can see broken branches of the hedge where the person forced their way through." Evelyn exclaimed. "It's a shame this track wasn't a dirt track, might have left some footprints or something."

David instinctively looked down to see if there were

any footprints, but there were no such marks on the hard tarmac surface. However, he did see a small dark, oily mark on the road.

With nothing else to report they headed back the way they came before walking back along the street to David's house. They could now see a police van parked outside the house with 'Forensics' written on the side. As they approached they could see a person dressed in a white oversuit and face mask walking out of the house, past Officer Smith who was still standing by the door. They were carrying a large suitcase full of equipment.

"Hello again. What are the chances, twice in one day!" the person in the white oversuit said.

"Sorry?" said David.

"Oh, forgive me." the person in the suit said. They took off the hood and mask and revealed their identity as Officer Danielle Thompson. "I'm so used to wearing this get up I forget others can't see me."

"Hello Danielle!" said Evelyn, glad to see a familiar face. "What's the news?"

"You don't hang around, do you Evelyn?" Danielle joked. "Well, there isn't much to tell to be honest, I didn't detect any fingerprints outside and I will use David's police record to rule out his fingerprints."

"I was wondering if you got a chance to look at the boxes in the kitchen? One of them had a black mark on it." David asked.

"You have a keen eye David." said Danielle, impressed. "Preliminary analysis indicates some kind of engine oil. I will know more when I get back to the lab and process the scene."

"Oh ok, I wonder how that got there?" David thought out loud.

"I guess that's your job to figure out." said Danielle with a smile.

"Now that you mention it, there was a similar mark on the track behind the house." David replied.

"Another good spot. I will go and take a sample to see if we have a match." Danielle commented. "By the way, Barksley called and said he has arranged for a locksmith to come and fix the window lock and upgrade your locks. Officer Smith will stay here until the locksmith has been and gone."

"That's great." David said, surprised. "I will have to thank him when we next see him."

Evelyn did not look so impressed. "It's the least he could do after this morning's interrogation."

"I completely understand, but Barksley has his moments. He is under a lot of pressure, so best to enjoy the good times whilst they last with him." Danielle replied.

The three stood there in silence for a few moments,

gathering their thoughts.

"So where next then David?" Evelyn asked, breaking the silence.

"Well, I think we need to get you back to Little-Astwick." David answered.

"I'm heading back that way. Still more to do at the Manor." Danielle commented. "I can give you a lift back if you like?"

"That would be great!" Evelyn replied enthusiastically.

"Hop in the van and you can show me what you found in the lane on the way." Danielle said as she pointed to her forensics van.

The three of them got into the van, David giving Officer Smith a sarcastic wave goodbye as they drove off. Officer Smith returned the wave with one hand, whilst taking another sip of coffee.

Chloe stood up, stretching her aching knees. She had only been doing the job for a few years, but was already aware of the demands of the job on her body. She walked around the tent, taking in the scene in front of her. She liked looking at a scene from a distance as a change of perspective. Ironically, she thought, you sometimes miss the details by looking too closely.

Danielle had been called to another scene. One of the local officers had their house broken into.

Chloe had made good progress, revealing the rest of the hand and forearm, as well as revealing the other hand too. She pressed the record button on the dictaphone once more.

"This is an unusual burial." Chloe said into her dictaphone. She stopped walking to look at the scene in more detail whilst she spoke. "Rather than the arms being by the side of the torso or even over the top of the torso, it appears that the arms are outstretched in front of the body, almost as if they are reaching up for something."

She turned off the dictaphone and crouched back down to continue her work, ensuring her knees were safely on the foam kneeling pad.

CHAPTER NINE

Danielle pulled the van over to the side of the road outside Evelyn's house. David and Evelyn got out and thanked Danielle for the lift before she drove off, heading back towards the Manor.

"Fancy a cuppa?" Evelyn asked as she walked towards her front door, unlocking it.

"That would be lovely!" David said, as he followed her in.

Evelyn walked into the kitchen to say hello to her dog Charlie, but Charlie walked straight past her and went to say hello to David. David gave him some fuss and stroked his head gently.

"Looks like you have made an impression on him." Evelyn said with a smile. "I'll put the kettle on."

Evelyn filled up the kettle with fresh water, then flicked the switch to start the water boiling. She then walked over to the back door and unlocked it, letting in some fresh air, Charlie running outside to the back garden to do his business. Evelyn carried on making the tea, getting the mugs out of the cupboard and putting a couple of tea bags into the teapot.

"Woof, woof!" Charlie barked from outside. Evelyn looked out the window, seeing Charlie barking in the direction of the fence at the back of the garden. She looked up and saw a flash of black disappear behind the fence. It was a bit of a blur, but she was sure it looked like the shape of a head and shoulders.

"David! There is someone at the back of the garden!" Evelyn shouted.

David ran out through the front door and headed around the outside of the house as fast as he could to the other side of the garden fence. Just before he rounded the corner, he stopped a second to catch his breath, then swung himself around the corner of the fence, ready for whatever he saw.

Except he wasn't ready to see absolutely nothing. There was no one there. The village street was empty. No one was running or walking away. He thought to himself, maybe Evelyn was just spooked and just thought she saw someone? Could it have been a cat?

He walked over to inspect the fence and couldn't see anything out of order. The fence was painted a dark brown colour, well looked after, the grass at its base well trimmed and maintained. The residents of this village were obviously very keen to maintain the high standards. He was about to walk back to Evelyn's house when he noticed a small patch of slightly darker wood. He leant closer to inspect it in more detail, suddenly realising it was the same colour as the mark left on the boxes in his kitchen. He took out his phone from his pocket and took a photo, then headed back into the house to tell Evelyn what he had found.

Evelyn stood at the front door, waiting for David to return.

"I couldn't see anyone there," David explained as he walked over to her. Evelyn looked disappointed, hoping David had apprehended the person. "But I did find something." David finished. Evelyn's face lit up in excitement. David didn't reply but he pointed inside the house. They both walked back inside to the house, shutting and locking the front door behind them out of an abundance of caution.

"The same dark mark that was on the box inside my house and the alley was on your back fence." David explained.

"It must be the same person?" Evelyn stated. "They couldn't find what they were looking for at your house so they tried to find it at mine."

David instinctively put his hand over his jacket

pocket, feeling the leather cylinder still there. He undid the jacket pocket and retrieved the object, showing it to Evelyn for the first time.

"That thing has caused a hell of a lot of trouble!" Evelyn exclaimed. "Time to open it and take a look."

David nodded in agreement and walked over to Evelyn's dining table, placing the object down on the surface, then took a seat. Evelyn turned the light on to help them see before joining David at the table.

He pulled on the loose thread a bit more, the thread coming all the way out from the leather cylinder. The circular lid piece fell out and David inserted his fingers, pulling the antique piece of paper from the cylinder, revealing it to the outside world for the first time in centuries. David carefully unrolled the yellowing paper, revealing a circular shape with an inner circle removed from the centre. There were various illustrations of leaves and trees, with some kind of roses.

There was some text written around the edge of the circular paper in a cursive script. David moved the circle around keeping the text the right way up as he read it aloud for Evelyn to hear.

To learn the secret,
Mind your manners,
You'll have to study,
For it won't come easy,
It's where you think,

But not where you think it is,
Where once good ideas are shelved,
There are no clouds with no sky,
But always ready for a rainy day.

"What the hell does that mean?" David asked.

"It's obviously a clue of some kind," Evelyn answered, "How are you at riddles?"

"I hate riddles, if they want us to know something then why don't they just tell us?"

David looked at the rest of the paper again. The edges of something were visible in the centre but it was not clear what it was, with the centre of the paper missing. There were some kind of claws visible on the right of the paper and a tail protruding from the left. He traced the outline of the drawing with his index finger, drawing Evelyn's attention.

"Do you remember the ring Alan found?" Evelyn asked.

"Oh yes, I wonder if this is the same animal that was on the ring?" David answered. "We should speak to George about this."

"The second line of the poem!" Evelyn started, before pausing, considering its meaning for a few seconds. "Do you think it could be a play on words? Manners, could be referring to George's Manor?

"Or multiple Manors?" David added.

"You'll have to study." Evelyn read the next line. "Could that be referring to the study in the house, or a library?"

"Yes, the room George went into when we left had shelves of books in it! Where you think!" David exclaimed.

"We need to get to the Manor!" Evelyn and David said in unison. David gently rolled the paper back up as it had been for the past centuries and slid it gently back into the leather cylinder, placing it back into his jacket pocket.

Evelyn and David stood up from the kitchen table, ready to go. They turned around and stopped in their tracks, their path blocked by Charlie looking up at them. The friendly dog had his lead in his mouth and his right paw raised up in the air, begging politely for a walk.

"Yes, of course you can come too." Evelyn said to Charlie, patting his head gently, before attaching the lead to the dog's collar. She locked up the back door to the garden, then the three of them left via the front door, locking that securely behind them too.

As soon as they left the house, Evelyn's neighbour, Mrs Francis, started talking to them from her front garden.

"Afternoon Evelyn. What's all this then?" Mrs Francis questioned. "First there was all the business at the church last night, now you got your police friend running around the streets too!"

"Oh, nothing to be concerned with Mrs Francis. Everything is under control." Evelyn smiled back, trying to act like it was just a normal day.

"Hmmm." Mrs Francis grunted, not looking convinced. They were about to walk off when Mrs Francis spotted the dog on the lead. "Oh, I'm glad you have decided to take your dog with you this time. He's been barking very loudly today."

David and Evelyn looked at each other, unsure what to say.

"I'm terribly sorry, but it was only for a short while." David replied.

"You call half an hour a short while? The barking was doing my head in whilst you were out. I could hardly hear today's episode of Bargain Hunt!" Mrs Francis replied gruffly.

"Oh, sorry I didn't know." replied Evelyn. "It's been a bit hectic today. Hopefully the walk now will calm Charlie down a bit."

"Yes. Hopefully." Mrs Francis walked back into her house, unconvinced.

The trio walked back into the village and past the church, heading for the path that Alan had informed them about earlier in the day so they could once more avoid the police in the field outside the manor.

They approached the street where Alan lived, walking past his old cottage. David noticed the garage doors were still open, but this time there was a classic MGB in orange sat there in the garage. The house looked empty from what he could see.

They took the path at the end of the street, letting Charlie off the lead so he could have a run around on their way. Evelyn attached the lead once more as they reached the end of the path. They emerged from the gap in the hedge, but this time there were police all around the manor house. They quickly returned to the cover of the hedge and poked their heads out, looking to see if they had been noticed. Luckily it seemed the police officers were more interested in the house than its surroundings.

They could see the forensics van belonging to Danielle outside the house, the back doors open, but they couldn't see Danielle. They assumed she must be inside the house, collecting evidence, but evidence of what they had no idea. Evelyn looked at David and they slid back into their hiding place in the hedge.

"What should we do?" Evelyn asked. "We need to get in the house!"

"I'm not sure how we can get in without them seeing us?" David replied.

They stood in silence for a few seconds, thinking.

Suddenly a smile emerged on Evelyn's face, an idea forming.

"How about you go over to them and find out what's going on, then I'll cause a distraction and we can sneak in?" Evelyn said.

"A distraction? What kind of distraction?" David asked, slightly concerned.

"That would ruin the surprise..." Evelyn said.

David shook his head side to side, then smiled back at Evelyn. Although he had only known Evelyn for a short while he knew to trust her and he knew when not to ask more questions.

David straightened his hat and jacket, ensuring his appearance was as tidy as it could be, then walked purposefully out of the gap in the hedge towards the crowd of police officers. He stopped at the nearest officer and tapped her on the shoulder.

"Good afternoon, Officer Grange," David said, reading the name on her badge, never having worked with her before. "I was in the area and just thought I'd see what was going on and if I could be of any assistance."

Officer Grange looked at the newcomer to the scene and assessed the new visitor, seeing his uniform she started to talk. "Morning. We had reports of blood found at the premises. Officer Barksley and some officers went in to investigate and arrest a suspect, but he is not coming quietly. Reinforcements were then called."

David had the pleasure of knowing George, aware he was a friendly caring soul, but also aware that he would not want to make him angry. He wondered how many officers it would take to arrest him, but before he could consider it in too much detail, a large throng of police officers emerged from the Manor's front door. They surrounded George, his hands handcuffed behind his back, a little blood running from a small cut on his forehead. David could see the wires from a taser dangling down from his back behind George, another officer holding the connected taser gun, ready to give him another shock if needed.

David instinctively walked closer to George to speak to him, before DI Barksley finally emerged from the house. A blood red tissue was rammed up his left nostril, his nose looking slightly misaligned from the last time he had seen him.

George looked around and saw David out of the corner of his eye, then immediately started shouting at David. "They are going to BOOK me David. BOOK me!"

"Shut up or we'll get that taser going again." DI Barksley shouted back angrily, before he stared at David whilst pointing to his right ear. David couldn't be sure, due to the distance and the crowd around him, but he was sure DI Barksley then subtly winked at him.

The police officers shuffled George towards a large police van, George finally complying and entering the van. The other officers looked around at each other, not wanting the short straw of sitting in the back of the van with George as they escorted him away.

DI Barksley shouted once more, "For heaven's sake!". He pushed his way through the crowd of officers and made his way into the back of the van, sitting next to George. The officers outside looked visibly relieved. One of the officers closed the van's doors and then walked to the van's cab and got in. The crowd moved away from the van, some going back into the house, others walking towards other police cars, their job at the scene now done.

The van slowly pulled away and headed down the lane with another 4 police cars going with it, leaving three more cars at the scene. David stood still, wondering what to do with himself, not having a role to play like the other officers. He started walking towards Danielle's van to see if he could spot her.

As he approached the van, he now wondered what Evelyn's plan was for her distraction.

He didn't have to wait long.

Chloe's eyes had started watering. Even though she was in the tent, the countryside air was still blowing gently through the holes at its base, letting the grass pollen in. She stood up and reviewed her progress, before clicking on her dictaphone once more.

"As initial indications showed, the body is facing south, not aligned east west like traditional burials. The positioning of the body still does not make any sense to me." Chloe reported.

She picked up the camera from the open case next to her, hooked the strap over her neck and then brought the eyepiece up to her right eye, squinting to look through it better. She blinked a couple of times, trying to force the water droplets from her eye to see clearer, but it was no use.

"Oh, hello!" came an unknown voice behind her. Chloe turned around, still holding the camera up to her right eye. A blurry figure, dressed in white appeared in the camera viewport, she zoomed in on the unknown face and instinctively clicked the button to take a photo. The next thing she saw was a hand reaching for the camera. It all went dark as it covered the lens.

She moved back from the camera at the same time as the figure pulled the camera away from her face. The heavy camera swung away from her, the camera strap limiting its distance, before coming back at her with force, impacting on her left temple. She fell to the ground.

Chloe was unconscious, but the recording dictaphone was still rolling. It recorded the sound of someone searching, opening cases of equipment, rifling through drawers, opening plastic bags. The noise suddenly stopped, the searched-for item now discovered.

"Help! Officer down, we need immediate assistance!" screamed the unknown figure into the recording, followed by a brief clinking metallic sound, then the plastic of the tent door moving as the figure walked out of the tent.

"Help! Officer down, we need immediate assistance!" came a voice from over the fence and the nearby field. One of the other officers called it in over their radio to call for an ambulance, the officers in the house hearing the call came out to look too, heading quickly for the field. David looked around and saw Evelyn and Charlie emerge from the bush and head towards the manor's front door as stealthily as they could, hoping none of the distracted officers caught sight of them.

Evelyn and Charlie crept in through the door, keeping an eye out for anyone left inside. David looked around, making sure the coast was clear for him too and trotted quickly inside after them.

The house was empty of people, but there had been a real commotion inside. Pieces of furniture had been moved and chairs were lying flat on the floor. At the bottom of the grand staircase there was now a pool of a thick, dark red congealed blood. They walked over to look closer, but heard a rustling sound coming from the front door. The trio stopped, then went into the living room, then into what they assumed to be the library, where George had run off to earlier, shutting the door as quietly as possible behind them.

David breathed a sigh of relief. Happy to finally have reached their target, but then a look of dread came over him as he turned to Evelyn.

"So that was your plan? Knock out a police officer?" David asked.

"What? That wasn't me!" Evelyn replied, her face forming an angry frown. "How dare you think I could do such a thing!"

"What?" David questioned, "But... wasn't that your distraction?"

"Oh..." Evelyn understood why David had come to that conclusion now. "Sorry. No, I didn't get a chance to do my distraction."

"Oh ok." David said, relieved. The relief only lasted for a moment until he realised that someone else must have injured the officer. "So who was it then?"

Evelyn shrugged, as Charlie pulled slightly on the lead as he headed towards the closed door. Evelyn put her finger over her mouth to signify David to keep quiet. She gave Charlie some fuss, hoping that he would be distracted enough not to bark and reveal their location. They heard the sound of rustling getting louder from the other side of the door, until the sound stopped. After about ten seconds, but what felt like an eternity to Evelyn and David, the rustling sound started again, but started getting quieter instead of louder this time, signifying it was moving away.

After a minute of silence, Evelyn spoke in hushed tones. "That rustling sound, it sounded like someone in one of those oversuits. It could be Danielle?"

"We can't take that risk, it could be anyone!" David replied. "But what about the injured officer?"

"We can't worry about the officer right now or poor George, we need to focus on what we are here for." Evelyn whispered back.

"Yes, I suppose so." David replied, also in a whisper. "Although I'm not sure what you mean by poor George. He seems to be able to handle himself well enough!"

David looked around the room, not spotting anything useful. They were in the library or study, in the room where you think. He thought about the next line of the poem they had discovered. It read, 'But not where you think it is'. Another super helpful clue, David thought, so he continued onto the next lines.

Where once good ideas are shelved,
There are no clouds with no sky,
But always ready for a rainy day.

"Where once good ideas are shelved." David said out loud to himself, thinking and looking around. "Well, there are plenty of shelves here, but where to look? Stupid riddles!"

Evelyn gave a quick smile back, then turned and looked around the room, taking in its features for the first time. The walls were covered in bookcases, with the only spaces for the door and the windows. There was a large wooden desk in the centre of the room, with a leather writing surface, also covered in books, but neatly stacked in piles as if they were in the process of being sorted. Unlike the others, one large book in the centre of the desk was wide open.

"What was George shouting at you just now?" Evelyn asked David.

"Nothing much, just saying the police had arrested him." David replied.

"What were his exact words?" Evelyn asked once more, still looking at the desk.

"Well, he said 'They were going to book him'." David

replied.

Evelyn went for a closer look at the open book. "I think he was giving us another clue." Evelyn spoke excitedly, before housing her voice back down to a whisper once more. "The one open book on the desk!"

David walked over to the desk and stood next to Evelyn as they read the page together.

'The house was built in the late 17th Century after being gifted to Arthur Androse as a part payment for the work he conducted at the nearby Lamport estate. The previous tenants owned a small farmhouse on the land with some out buildings that housed the animals. Upon discovering that the previous tenants had been evicted, Arthur Androse purchased a small cottage in the nearby village of Little-Astwick for the tenants to live in and rehired them to manage the farm on his behalf.'

There was a diagram of the house below the text. They both recognised the style of the drawings as the same as the pictures of the church they had seen the previous day. They moved onto the next page of the book and continued reading.

'Androse designed the house himself, an accomplished architect in his own right. There are some that say his design was much simpler than his other buildings, but there were rumours that the architectural gems of the house were not in plain sight.'

'After ten years of living in the house, he left the country to design a grand house for a relative in America, but he never managed to return back to his home. There was speculation that he passed away in the Americas, but it was never confirmed. There was also speculation that his boat never made it across the Atlantic ocean, with others speculating that he never even made it onto the boat in the first place.'

'After five years with no word or sighting Arthur Androse was declared legally dead. He did not have any children and his wife was unable to inherit his estate and had no other family that could either. His will stipulated that upon his death, the estate should transfer to a Mr Godfrey Warwick, the original tenants of the farmland the house is built upon. Mr Warwick repaid the kindness that Androse had shown him, allowing Arthur's wife, Mary, to live in the house until the end of her days. Godfrey Warwick's eldest grandchild, also named Godfrey, then moved into the house with his new wife Jessica.'

'Although this seemed like a happy ending to the story, it was fraught with trouble. The owners of the Lamport estate made many legal claims against the property, stating that it should return back to the Templeton family as the will was invalid. The Templeton family lost every legal challenge they made, eventually having to desist due to expensive court fees and a lack of collateral to settle their accounts.'

"That's a sad story about Androse and his wife."

Evelyn commented, "But nice that they gave the house back to the original tenants of the land. I wonder if George is related to them?"

David turned the page over and as if by magic there was a family tree detailing the Warwick family line, ending with Godfrey George Warwick, the only child. David had a hunch that George was using his middle name rather than his real first name and that was him in the family tree. The dates seemed to match pretty well too.

"So Androse designed and built this house too, just like the church!" David said, thinking back about what they had just read.

"This clue, it must open a passageway like in the church." Evelyn said, her eyes wide with excitement.

David flipped the page back and looked at the diagram of the house once more. Unlike the church blueprints, this diagram didn't have any secret rooms on it that they could see. He looked at the pile of books on the desk, trying to spot anything that stood out in the book titles but nothing seemed out of the ordinary. He thought about the poem lines again.

Where once good ideas are shelved,
There are no clouds with no sky,
But always be ready for a rainy day.

"What do you need to be ready for a rainy day?" David asked.

"A coat, a hat, an umbrella?" Evelyn replied, looking around the room. She saw a tall hatstand in the corner of the room and walked over to it. "Could it be this?" She took a deep breath and then pulled the tall hatstand like a long lever, expecting it to trigger some kind of mechanism.

But nothing happened.

The hatstand was completely freestanding, no connection to any other mechanisms. She looked closer and saw a well known 20th Century furniture brand stamped on the dark tubular metal, then rolled her eyes in disappointment.

"Nice thinking, what else could it be? Did they have umbrellas back then?" David asked. He got his phone out of his pocket and searched for when umbrellas were invented. The top result said 1852, halfway through the 19th century, much too late, but then he scrolled down a bit further and read the next result that said umbrellas had been invented 4,000 years ago. The first result was talking about more modern steel ribbed umbrellas.

"Yes, it could be an umbrella of some kind, they were invented a long time ago!" David said, putting his phone back into his pocket.

Evelyn looked around the room once more and spotted a light fitting in the ceiling above the desk. The metal came down from the ceiling, becoming wider, then tapering once more, then curving at the bottom like an umbrella handle. She climbed up onto the top of the desk and reached for the light fitting. She pushed it gently seeing if it would move in any direction, the brass cold to the touch.

It didn't move.

She lowered herself down from the desk, before lowering herself back onto the floor.

"I guess this is where the super helpful line 'But not where you think it is' comes into play." David joked, Evelyn not seeing the funny side.

David looked at the shelves once more, wondering where the books had come from that were now on the desk. He saw a shelf with a few spaces in it and headed over to it.

He read the spines of the books left on the shelf. Most were about horticulture and architecture, but one book looked different. The outer was old embossed leather like the others, the pages were old paper, but very uniform, very neat and tidy unlike the well worn pages of the other books, almost as if it had never been read. The golden writing along the spine was worn with time but he could still read it, "The road to hell is paved with good intentions" and underneath was some kind of long thin symbol.

"This could be it!" David said with excitement. Evelyn had an expression on her face that showed she was yet to be convinced after the last two attempts had ended in failure, but she walked over to where David was standing to get a closer look.

David carefully pulled the book out from the shelf, hoping he had found the trigger. The book moved freely, too freely to be attached to any kind of lever, but he kept going just in case, hoping that he would suddenly hear a loud clunk and clicking sound, revealing its secret to them.

But there was nothing.

David now had the book in his hand, fully out of the shelf. No connection to any mechanism in sight. But the book was definitely not an ordinary book. It felt heavier than other books its size and it would not open.

"Maybe the answer is inside the book?" David questioned. "Should we try and break it open?"

David handed the book to Evelyn whilst he searched the room for something he could use to force the book open. He looked around the desk for anything sharp. Evelyn, meanwhile, looked more closely at the symbol under the text on the spine of the book. The gold had worn away from most of the pattern, the long thin strip of gold the only piece remaining.

She walked over to the window to get a bit more light. Once there she held the spine up to the light, seeing a shadow of the original embossed symbol. She recognised the shape, but it was upside down. An upside down umbrella.

David looked over his shoulder and saw Evelyn focusing on the book by the window. He gave up his hunt for something sharp and walked back over, intrigued as to what she had found.

"What is it?" David asked.

"But always be ready for a rainy day." Evelyn replied.

David reached for the book to see for himself, but Evelyn held her other hand up, indicating to give her a moment longer. She moved the book back to the empty slot where the book had come from, but before she put it back, she flipped it over so the writing was upside down and the umbrella symbol was now the correct way up.

She held her breath as she slid the book back into position on the shelf. As it reached the back of the bookcase, just as David had before, she prepared herself for a large clunking noise or a series of clicks, or even a rush of stale air as a secret passageway was forced open releasing air that had been trapped for centuries.

Instead there was a very faint, very short click, as the bookcase moved a few millimetres indicating a lock had been released. Evelyn let out her breath.

"Well that was a bit anticlimactic." David stated.

"Maybe this was designed to be quiet so it could be used more often?" Evelyn shrugged. And with that she pulled on the bookshelf to see if it would open further. The bookcase moved with surprising ease with the weight of the books on it, but unfortunately it released an extremely loud creaking noise as it moved, the old hinges lacking any kind of lubrication from years of desuetude.

David and Evelyn looked back to the door that they entered the room from, expecting someone to barge through, but no one came. Then they heard the rustling sound once more, getting louder as it moved closer to the door!

Evelyn grabbed the book that had opened the passageway and turned it back upright, reinserting it into the bookshelf, before heading into the newly revealed passageway, pulling David in with her. She made a short, quiet, whistling noise and Charlie ran in after them. The bookcase door swung shut behind them with another loud creak.

CHAPTER TEN

David, Evelyn and Charlie stood in complete darkness, wondering if entering the passageway had been such a great idea after all. David retrieved his phone from his pocket and activated the torch. The light was blinding after a few seconds of pitch black. He swung the torch around in a wide arc, revealing their surroundings in a bit more detail.

The room had a level floor, with stone walls, the same dark ironstone as the exterior walls of the house, and a flat smooth ceiling. David moved his torch back to examine the floor in more detail. It did seem to have a faint join down the middle. He got down onto his knees, feeling along the edge of the join, hoping for a mechanism trigger of some kind.

Evelyn got her phone out too and looked at the screen. Charlie sat quietly at her feet, unsure why they wanted to go in the dark room. No phone signal. Not really surprising. She thought back to the second half of the poem, hoping it would reveal some more clues.

It's where you think,
But not where you think it is,
Where once good ideas are shelved,
There are no clouds with no sky,
But always ready for a rainy day.

"But not where you think it is…" Evelyn said, seeing David looking around the floor. If you were looking for a way down you would think to look at the floor. With the line of the poem in her head she started looking up, using her torch to illuminate the low smooth ceiling. She couldn't see anything in particular, but then as she moved the torch away, she was sure she saw a faint flash of some kind. She moved the torch over the area once more, but there was nothing there, but as she moved her torch away a flash of something appeared briefly again.

"David, do you see this?" Evelyn asked. David looked up from his crouched position and shone his torch up to the ceiling, trying to see what Evelyn was looking at.

"I can't see anything?" David answered.

"Turn your torch off." Evelyn said, excited.

"What?" He questioned, not understanding.

"Just do it, trust me!" Evelyn pleaded. David complied and turned his torch off. As he did so, they both saw a little flash of a small shape in the ceiling. Evelyn moved her torch back over the area, then away again, repeating the motion. David stood and raised his hand, moving his fingers closer to where the light had emitted from. Once he found the spot, he looked closer and could see a flash of a sun shape.

"There are no clouds with no sky." Evelyn said, seeing the sun shape now.

David pushed the shape gently, its surface completely smooth but it moved up ever so slightly. Another small click noise sounded and Evelyn shone her torch around to try and find where it came from. The small crack in the floor was now slightly higher on one side than previously. David bent back down and put his fingers under the gap and lifted up the section of floor, hinging upwards from the wall side, this time the hinges were almost silent. Evelyn's torch revealed another spiral staircase downward.

David pushed the section of floor over until it rested against the adjacent wall. He started walking down the stairs, one by one with Evelyn following, Charlie walking behind the pair of them. One step, two steps, three steps, four steps, five...

Memories of the previous day suddenly flashed before Evelyn's eyes. She reached out and grabbed David's jacket pulling him back towards her to safety, just as the fifth step hinged downwards. David screamed out in surprise.

He turned to Evelyn and thanked her for saving him. "Thank you Evelyn! I owe you one!"

They proceeded down the staircase with extra caution. The stairs winding their way down at least five metres.

Once at the bottom, Evelyn shone her torch to reveal another empty room. The room had ironstone walls, with a flagstone floor, the ceiling held up by large oak beams spanning the cavity. The room was about five metres long and two metres wide.

"What is it with these empty rooms?" David asked.

But before Evelyn could answer, a voice emerged from the darkness behind them. David, Evelyn and Charlie turned and instinctively stepped back from the opening of the staircase and further into the room.

"Thank you for paving the way for me." came the voice. "I have spent many years searching for this secret and you stumbled upon it in a matter of hours!"

Evelyn shone her torch slowly along the floor arching towards the doorway, illuminating a set of shoes, then a pair of legs, then a tool belt with various tools clipped on. Recognising the belt, Evelyn moved the torch quickly up to reveal the face both Evelyn and David recognised.

"Alan? What are you doing here?" David asked, surprised to see him.

Alan stepped forward into the light. In his left hand he had an oversuit that the forensic officers were wearing outside. He threw the white suit down onto the floor by his side.

"Fifth step. The doctors said that's all that Michelle kept mumbling as she flowed in and out of consciousness." Alan remarked. "I was glad of the warning."

Alan interlaced his fingers and stretched them out in front of him, warming up for his story. "It's a long tale, so I'd appreciate not being interrupted this time and ruining the ending." Alan smirked at them. "And to motivate you to keep your mouths shut, I have my incentive right here."

Alan put his right hand behind his back and slowly moved it back out in front of him, revealing a large pickaxe with a long wooden handle and a sharp point on the end of the metal pick.

David thought back to his training, opening his mouth, about to see if he could de-escalate the situation before it got any more serious. Before he could even begin, Alan swung the pickaxe in front of him in the space between them.

"I warned you. Don't push me." Alan retorted.

Evelyn and David took another step back out of caution. Charlie stood his ground and gave a little growl. For a second, a flash of fear appeared over Alan's face, before he quickly restored his confident smirk. Even though it was a split second, Evelyn had noticed. She had seen a similar look on the postman's face before Charlie and the postman got to know each other.

"You already know the legend of the missing Templeton fortune, having the pleasure of hearing the story earlier today." Alan started, letting the pickaxe rest on the floor, his point made and his confidence coming through now he was talking. "Michelle is the last of that proud family line, and she knew of my interest in the legend, so she asked me for assistance."

"She knew there was something in the church and she was moments away from finding it, until you two ruined her carefully orchestrated plan. She was smart enough to know that her plan may not work and made contingency plans. Someone to carry out her orders in her stead. But to catch up to the present day, first we need to go back in time."

"Arthur Androse was employed by the Templeton family as their architect for their estate. As part of the contract he organised for this land to be handed over to him, but the original deal was supposed to be temporary, allowing him to live near the estate whilst work was being completed."

Alan looked at his nails on his right hand as he spoke, completely relaxed, feeling in complete control of the situation. David and Evelyn remained silent as Alan spoke.

"But then there were murmurs and rumours circling around London that the Templeton family were in financial difficulty." Alan paused for effect before shouting, "FALSE RUMOURS!"

Alan continued in his calm voice once more, his point made. "The rumours were started by Androse, spreading lies among the elite in the capital. Why you may ask? To extort additional money from the Templeton family."

"He started with black mailing money, then he moved to property, getting the deeds for this very house and land. But then he went too far and forced Sir William Templeton to hand over his family signet ring. The very symbol of his family estate and history."

"Was that the ring you found today?" Evelyn asked.

"I said NO INTERRUPTIONS!" Alan said, picking up the pickaxe once more with both hands, holding it in front of him this time to maintain his threat. His eyes were bulging with rage at the disrespect he had been shown.

Evelyn put her index finger over her mouth, indicating she understood to stay silent whilst

David raised his hands in front of him in surrender.

Alan took a few breaths, steadying himself before continuing his story, the pickaxe remaining in front of him, ready to strike when needed. After he had composed himself, he started talking once more. "Yes, that was the ring. I finally had it in my hand, but I was not prepared for discovering the bones. I won't be making that mistake again!"

Alan released his left hand from the tight grip on the pickaxe. It lowered slightly as he did so. He put his left hand into his left trouser pocket and retrieved something. He opened his hand to show David and Evelyn the ring. "And now I have the ring back once more. Ready to return it to its rightful owners, the Templeton family. You already know their last descendent, Michelle, but I am also a descendant…" he paused, thinking carefully about how to explain this statement. "You see, my name may not be on the family tree, but my family have always been loyal to the Templetons, providing support throughout the years and they have been as loyal to us. My family is also part of the bloodline, just not recognised through official channels."

"Michelle has agreed to share the lost treasure with me, splitting it evenly to reward my family's years of loyal service."

David and Evelny looked at each other, understanding that one of Alan's ancestors was born out of wedlock to the Templeton family. They looked back at Alan as he continued talking once more. David was about to sigh, feeling fed up with this long monologue, wondering when it was about to end. However, he didn't want to risk upsetting Alan again, so he kept his thoughts to himself.

"A previous attempt was made to retrieve this ring. Sir William Templeton did not attempt this himself, but his younger brother Edward was proud and knew what the ring meant to the family. Edward told his brother he would return the ring to its rightful owners, but his attempt failed. After his misadventure the family sent him away to live in the north of England."

Alan's left eyebrow raised slightly as he paused for thought, before continuing. "Today, I have been thinking over who the bones must belong to." A smile slowly appeared across his mouth as he spoke, "Then I realised, it must be the bones of the traitor Androse. Buried in a pauper's grave! A fitting end for a liar and a thief!"

"But let's catch up to modern day. To have time to look properly through the library and find the treasure I had to get that oaf George out of the way. Smashing his window and pouring blood all over the floor was easy enough to get the police to take him away. What I didn't count on was the call for reinforcements."

"A little imagination and improvisation got around

that. Dressing up as a forensic allowed me free reign of the site, then a little distraction knocking out one of the other forensics, who just happened to have a pickaxe with them. Calling 'officer down' emptied the house and let me... and you... straight in."

Alan cackled an evil laugh, swinging his head back in enjoyment.

Evelyn ceased her chance and took a step forward, Charlie standing in front of her, protecting his owner. Charlie started growling once more.

Alan immediately stopped laughing and looked back towards Evelyn and Charlie, a look of panic replacing his smug smile. He took a small step backwards towards the entrance to the room.

"You are stupid to think that Michelle would share anything with you! She has been using you, just like her family has been using your family for centuries!" Evelyn stated confidently, taking another step forward towards Alan. David was worried for his friend's safety, but he stood still, knowing not to get in Evelyn's way in her moment of brilliance. He knew she wouldn't go down without a fight. "You know who the bones really belong to don't you?"

Alan, now feeling threatened, lifted the pickaxe above his head with his right hand, trying to steady it with his left hand which still had the ring in it.

"You and I both know that those bones belong

to Edward Templeton." Evelyn shouted at Alan, leaning her head and shoulders forward for greater effect. "The bones have been in the ground for over 200 years! He stole the ring, but something happened to him whilst he tried to escape! He was a thief that failed and the family lied to protect their own interests!"

"No... it's not true. It's not!" Alan started, his right hand trembling from the weight of the suspended pickaxe.

"You know it's true. Michelle is only interested in herself, just like the rest of her family! She won't share anything with you! She is using you!" Evelyn goaded, taking another half a step forward. Alan instinctively took another half step backwards.

David looked down at the floor where Alan had been standing moments before. There was a small black mark on the floor. The same black mark that he had seen in his house on the boxes and on Evelyn's garden fence.

"It was you! You broke into my house and tried to get into Evelyn's house too!" David screamed in anger, pointing to the black mark on the floor. Another realisation clicked in his mind, "And I bet your car backfires when it starts. That was the bang that was heard!"

Alan looked down, seeing the indisputable evidence that had given him away, taking one more step backwards.

"Yes, it was me. Who'd have thought it would be a classic British car that would give me away. I should have fixed that oil leak!" Alan admitted, his frustration showing through his voice. " I knew you had found something in the church. I couldn't find it at your house so I went to Evelyn's house. Your dog wouldn't let me get near it, kept barking at me, I was worried your neighbour would come to investigate. Luckily it seemed she was only worried about her TV program, so I left a listening device on your dog's collar to hear what you were saying."

"That's how you followed us here?" David surmised.

"Yes, then I heard you in the study and how you solved the riddle." Alan sneered at them. "Now, I'm the one with the weapon, you will do as I say. Give me the clue you found in the church or I'll take it off you by force!"

David and Evelyn both looked each other in the eye, Charlie still growling at Alan. They had a sudden moment of understanding between them without a word being spoken. They turned back to Alan and shouted "NO!" in unison, Charlie barking once in agreement.

Alan had finally had enough, his arms trembling and eyes bulging with rage from the lack of respect he had been shown. "Who do you think you are! I am a member of the Templeton family!"

He swung the pickaxe behind him, ready to swing it down towards Evelyn and David, but the double pointed pickaxe would not swing forward. He tried again, pulling with his right hand, but it would not budge. He turned to look, seeing the point now embedded in the old wooden roof beam.

In panic, he dropped the ring from his left hand as he grabbed the pickaxe handle with both hands, pulling the handle as hard as he could. The ring bounced on the floor, heading behind David into the corner of the room. Suddenly, a cracking sound emerged from the wooden beam as it splintered around the point of the pickaxe, freeing it. Alan turned back to Evelyn once more, ready to strike, but the cracked beam made another creak, before it split along the fault line created by previously stuck pickaxe.

Alan turned back around once more to look at the beam, seeing it splitting, creaking under the pressure, moving slowly downwards in a jarring motion, bit by bit, the rest of the ceiling around it vibrating with each movement. He looked over his shoulder at Evelyn, Charlie and David, weighing up his options, then ran for the entrance.

As he ran, the old wooden beam gave way, splitting fully along the crack, the ceiling following along with it. A wave of stones, dirt and dust followed, blocking Evelyn and David's view, unable to see what happened to Alan.

Evelyn, David and Charlie jumped backwards into the recess of the empty room, trying to get as far away from the collapse as possible.

The noise of crashing rocks continued for a few more seconds, until the cavity had been completely filled, the room now completely dark. David used his hands to feel the world around him. His fingers touched something cold and metal, realising it was the ring. He picked it up and put it in his jacket pocket, then continued to feel what else was there. Next he felt another object, this one flat and mostly smooth, until he reached a sharp piece that cut his finger. He felt around the edges and recognised a button, his mind recognising the outline of a smartphone. He lifted it up and what was left of the room was suddenly filled with a flash of light, the smartphone's torch still active, even with the screen cracked.

David looked around, seeing the pile of rubble blocking their exit, dust hanging in the air, settling slowly down towards the ground. He swung the torch in the opposite direction. He could now see Evelyn slumped in the corner, with Charlie, her loyal pet, licking her face gently.

Evelyn moved her head slightly to the left, her eyes still shut, a smile appearing on her face. "Andre…" Evelyn whispered. Despite the gravity of their situation, David couldn't help but laugh.

Evelyn heard the laughter, her eyes instantly popping open, adjusting to the light levels then looking around, seeing Charlie right in front of her and David lying on the floor. She sat up slowly, Charlie taking a step back, letting her move more freely.

"What's so funny?" Evelyn finally said to David.

"Nevermind, I'll tell you later." David replied, a smile still on his face but the laughter stopped. David now tried to sit up, but something twinged when he tried to move his left leg, searing pain shooting up from his foot all the way to his hip. Eveln saw David was in pain from the look on his face.

"Probably just twisted something." David spoke calmly despite the pain. "Could you give us a hand up?"

Evelyn got up slowly, shaking her head to knock away the cobwebs, then walked over to where David was laying, giving him a hand to help him stand. He was able to stand on both feet, as long as he kept the majority of weight on his right leg.

"Well, I don't think anything is broken." David said, putting on a fake smile to ease his friend's concerns. David shone the torchlight back over to the pile of rubble, the dust settling a bit more with every minute that passed. "Now we just need to find a way out of here."

David gave the cracked smartphone back to Evelyn to hold, then he got his own out of his pocket, turning the torch back on. They both looked for ways out but couldn't see anything.

He saw the pickaxe handle on the floor, amazingly covered in only a few stones. He bent down and lifted the pickaxe up. David tried to move some stone from the top of the rubble pile, but it was too heavy for him to move, even with the pickaxe. He dropped the useless tool to the ground.

Now the dust had settled a bit more, he noticed some steel wires hanging down, recently severed by the collapsed ceiling.

"Maybe these wires had something to do with getting out of here?" David said as he tried pulling on the dangling wire, but nothing happened. Dejected, he made his way back to the wall of the room and rested on it, taking the weight off his sore leg.

"So I guess we aren't going anywhere for a while then." David said. Evelyn was still waving her torch around trying to spot anything she could. "So, whilst we've got some time, why don't you tell me your plan for the distraction earlier."

Evelyn stopped what she was doing and looked down at the floor. She started laughing to herself, then said. "Forget it. It was a stupid idea."

David couldn't help but smile back, but he wanted to

know so he persisted. "Come on, you can tell me."

Evelyn looked at David. "You promise you won't laugh?" she asked. David nodded, the small smile still on his face. She rolled her eyes at him, then took a deep breath before continuing.

"Well, Charlie and I play this game at home. I hide his toy and he has to find it. Sometimes we play with an old bone, so I thought I could point at the tent in the field and he would go and find one of the bones, grab it and run away with it..." Evelyn stopped talking and started laughing, before adding, "It's so stupid now I say it out loud.", Evelyn and David both laughing together.

"I have to agree, that would have been one hell of a distraction!" David laughed back even though he said he wouldn't. "Officers running around chasing a dog with a bone!"

"Woof!" Charlie barked, hearing the word bone.

"Oh, now he thinks we are playing the game." Evelyn said. "Come here Charlie!"

But Charlie didn't come to Evelyn. Instead he walked over to a piece of wall between Evelyn and David and started scratching it with his paws, whimpering at the same time.

David walked over to where Charlie was scratching the wall, leaning against the wall as he went. "What have you got there Charlie? Is there a bone there?"

"Woof!" came the reply.

David, leaning against the wall, lost his balance slightly and thudded against the wall directly over Charlie. "Did you hear that?" David asked Evelyn.

"Hear what?" Evelyn replied.

"Listen!" David said as he fell against the wall once more, a gentle thud returning. He then moved a step backwards and fell against the wall once more. This time the thud sounded different. More solid somehow.

"You know what I was going to say before we were interrupted by Alan?" David asked. "I was watching a program about ancient Egypt the other week. They used to build these fake chambers so grave robbers would think that the grave had already been robbed. But these rooms were decoys, with the real burial room located behind the fake room. Can you give me a hand?"

David and Evelyn both started shoulder barging the piece of wall that gave the different sound. Over and over again they hit the ironstone brick wall with their shoulders until it eventually started moving. The stones seemed to be hinged, moving slightly inwards at an angle in the centre.

"Those wires must have been part of a mechanism to open this up!" David exclaimed. "If we can get it moving a bit more we might be able to squeeze through!"

Suddenly motivated by making some progress, they leaned back away from the wall and then heaved their shoulders into the wall as hard as they could. The hinged wall mechanism finally gave way, the ironstone blocks fully hinged open from each side and the couple fell through the magically appearing gap with a thud, landing on the cold ground of another room.

Charlie walked nonchalantly past them, before returning to Evelyn a few moments later with a long bone in his mouth.

CHAPTER ELEVEN

Officer Smith had caught a lift back to the Manor with the locksmith after ensuring David's house was secure. Danielle had seen him get out the van and started heading to a nearby police car.

"Where do you think you are going?" Danielle said.

"Sorry, what?" Officer Smith replied. "I'm off to get some coffee. I've been nothing but a glorified security guard recently and I need a break."

"You can get a coffee..." Danielle started, "Once we are finished here. And as you are so good at being a glorified security guard you can stand guard over Chloe and make sure no one goes near her. Understood."

Officer Smith looked at her, his mouth twitching, just willing to talk back and disobey a direct order. Instead he grunted and walked off into the field to carry out his new protection detail. Danielle headed into the manor house.

David and Evelyn were laying inches away from each other in the dark room, Charlie stood nearby still holding the long bone in his mouth. David and Evelyn laid still for a moment, the pain in their shoulders still raw from falling to the ground. They looked at each other, their faces partially lit by the light from their phones. They were wincing from the pain at first, but then smiling at each other from the thought of being free from the first room. They hugged each other for a few moments in celebration.

Evelyn stood first, then gave David a lift up, his left leg still causing him some pain. They circled the light from their phones around the room, lighting up the darkness. The room was slightly larger than the previous room, but it was finished in a similar manner, cold stone floors, ironstone walls and a ceiling held up with the wooden beams again. This room however, was not empty.

There was an open box on the left hand wall, its lid resting against the ironstone walls and one of the flagstone floor tiles had been lifted up. David walked over to take a look, shining his torch light down. Unlike the church, there was nothing in this storage space.

"It's empty." David said disappointedly. He shone his

torch around the edges of the flagstone. He felt the edges. Where they should have been smooth, there were tool marks and chips in the stone. David spoke out loud, thinking to himself. "It looks like someone has forced this open?"

Evelyn walked over to the wooden box and shone her torch on it. It was an exact copy of the small piano that was contained in the church's secret room.

"Maybe they didn't have the musical notes to open the secret flagstone?" Evelyn remarked. "Just used brute force to get to it?"

"Yes, that makes sense." David replied, but then a thought occurred to him. "When we triggered the secret flagstone, it also opened the door to get out? How did the people in here get out?"

They both shone their torches around the room, illuminating the far end of the room that had been in darkness until then.

The pristine ironwork blocks had been removed in a small section of the far wall, revealing a start of a hand dug passageway, just about wide enough for a person to fit through. A pile of soil was placed next to the blocks that had been removed from the wall.

Also on the floor was some old fabric. They looked like a pair of old breeches, except they were not empty. They had an assortment of bones, one tibia bone sticking out from one leg of the old trousers, the other tibia missing.

"Well, I guess we know where Charlie got the bone from." David winced in disgust.

"Uhh, Charlie... Drop that please!" Evelyn ordered. Charlie lovingly obliged and Evelyn patted him on the head. "Good boy!"

David moved closer to the hole in the wall and saw some more of the skeleton further into the tunnel, its hip bones still in situ, along with a pair of boots closer to the wall. From the waist up the skeleton was buried in soil.

"I think this was the plan to escape." David contemplated the fate of this person, wondering how long they were trapped in the darkness before they tried to dig their way out of the chamber, not being able to open the mechanism to escape with whatever they had found. Digging a tunnel with their bare hands before the tunnel collapsed in on them, buying them alive. He shuddered at the thought.

"Do you think we could get out this way?" Evelyn questioned.

"Well, it didn't work for the last person who tried, but I can't see any other way out?" David replied, trying to remove thoughts of being buried alive from running through his head.

Evelyn looked into the hole. "Maybe if we make it

bigger somehow?" she said, thinking out loud. "Oh I know!". She ran back into the previous room and grabbed the pickaxe from next to the pile of rubble, then ran back to David and Charlie.

"Stand back!" Evelyn ordered David. He was about to insist he did the digging, but after twisting to face her, his leg gave a sudden twinge of pain so he quickly gave up on that idea.

Evelyn started digging the hole a bit bigger, using the pickaxe to loosen the soil then scoop it away by hand. Charlie saw what she was doing and thinking it was another game, he helped dig away the soil with his little paws.

David stood and watched for a bit, then looked around the room again. He looked down at the old trousers on the floor and noticed there was a bulge in the otherwise flat material. He bent down and patted it, then patted his own jacket pocket. The shapes and sizes were identical. He picked up the material, the old bones finally slipping out the leg holes and onto the floor.

"Sorry!" David said instinctively, knowing very well the owner of the bones was well past complaining. He opened the pocket and pulled out another leather cylinder. It looked identical to the first one. He placed it in his jacket pocket with the leather cylinder from the church.

"Don't worry, I'm more than capable!" Evelyn

replied, facing away from David, her head in the hole.

"What?" David asked.

"You don't need to be sorry." Evelyn said. "I'm more than capable of digging a hole. Just because you're a man, doesn't mean that you have to do the hard work."

"Oh no I was saying sorry to the poor fellow buried alive." David explained.

Evelyn stopped digging for a moment thinking, then continued digging. "I think you may have hit your head as well as your leg." Evelyn jested. "We will get you checked over as soon as we are out of here."

Evelyn was digging near the skeleton, but trying not to disturb it, as well as trying not to cause another cave in.

Danielle had now finished her work in the manor house, analysing the blood. Her initial analysis showed the blood was animal blood and not human. She had also found traces of it on a smashed window. She was packing up her van, putting all the equipment away. It had been a busy day, as it always was for her, but her colleague being injured was a step too far. She would ensure she would use all her skills to figure out who had done that to her.

Luckily the damage was mostly superficial, patched up by a paramedic who attended the scene. Danielle had told her to go home and have a few days off, but Chole wanted to finish off the job and ensure the skeleton was wrapped up before they continued the next day.

Danielle grabbed a large thermos flask from the back of her van, along with three mugs, Officer Smith now having earned a cup of coffee along with her and Chloe. She walked into the field and towards the tent. Officer Smith was standing guard as she had ordered. She pulled back the plastic of the tent to look inside, Chloe was tidying everything up and putting away all their tools into the various cases.

Danielle dropped the plastic tent sheet back down and handed Officer Smith two mugs, before removing the lid from the thermos flask and pouring out two cups of coffee, one for him and one for Chloe.

She poured herself a cup then put the lid back on the thermos flask, placing it on the ground when she was finished. She took one of the mugs from Officer Smith and then said, "Would you mind?", indicating to the plastic sheet of the tent.

Officer Smith lifted the plastic, seeing the skull of the skeleton that had been carefully revealed throughout the day by Danielle and Chloe. Chloe stood up and took the coffee mug from Danielle, smiling and nodding in appreciation.

A high pitched scream of terror came out of Officer Smith.

Danielle and Chloe looked at his white ashen face, the colour having drained from it, mouth wide open aghast. He was looking at the skeleton. The two women followed his eyeline, turning to look at the skeleton.

"I swear the skull was on its side just now." Chloe commented calmly. "Now it's facing upwards?"

Before they could say anymore, the skull moved again, nodding gently up and down. It moved once more, before sinking back down to its original position. Then it moved so far forward that it tumbled from its location it had been in for the past centuries and in its place was a human hand pushing through the gap in the soil.

"ARRRGGHHHHHH!" came another high pitched scream from Officer Smith before he dropped both the coffee and the plastic sheet and ran as fast as he could. The other officers at the scene looked on in confusion.

"Ahh, is that you Danielle?" came a voice from the small hole where the skull had once been. "Any chance you could give us a hand to get out of here?"

Danielle and Chloe jumped into action, grabbing their shovels instead of their tiny brushes and trowels they would normally use for their precision work. Soon the hole was big enough for Evelyn, David and Charlie to emerge from.

"This has definitely been a day to remember!" Chloe said to the now crowded tent.

"Yes indeed." Danielle replied. "Don't get your hopes up, they are not all like this!"

"Thank god for that!" Chloe replied, smiling.

CHAPTER TWELVE

The three women, David and Charlie the dog, were sitting in the large kitchen of the manor house, the kettle boiling slowly on the worktop. A teapot with tea bags was ready to receive the water once it had boiled.

David had been looked over by the paramedic on scene and had strapped up his leg. The diagnosis was confirmed, nothing broken, just a sprain. He sat in a wooden arm chair, resting his leg as best he could. The others sat at an old wooden table in the corner of the kitchen waiting for the kettle to boil, chatting away about their adventurous day.

Knock, knock, knock.

Someone knocked on the door of the kitchen but didn't wait for it to be answered, they walked straight in.

"Ah so here you all are! Sitting down on the job I see!" DI Barksley said, looking slightly worse for wear. The tissue had been removed from his nose, but there was still a small amount of dried blood under his left nostril. A large bruise had started appearing around his left eye.

The kettle clicked off, having finally finished boiling. Danielle went to get up, but Barksley held up his hands insisting, "Allow me."

He went over to the kettle and filled up the large teapot with boiling water. He then got another two cups out from the kitchen cupboard as another person walked into the kitchen.

David instantly recognised the towering figure of George walking into the room, a look of menace on his face. David looked at the others in the room, expressions of panic on their faces after the last time they had seen Barksley and George together. George growled a deep beastly growl of anger, before his face suddenly transformed into a large smile.

"Ah ha ha!" George laughed at the room. "Got ya!"

A look of confusion spread across everyone's faces except Barksley. They looked to him for an explanation.

"We had an anonymous tip off that there was a crime scene inside the manor. So I thought I had better handle it myself." Barksley began. "But the Chief insisted I take a team with me. George and I know each other. Used to be good friends. We used to play rugby together in fact."

"Used to!" replied George.

"Yes used to," Barksley paused for a moment in acknowledgement, "Until one day I accidentally broke George's nose with a slightly misjudged tackle."

"Misjudged! That's putting it mildly!" George commented.

"Yes, indeed. So George had said that next time he saw me he would repay the favour." Barksley said.

"And I upheld my promise!" George stated matter of factly.

"Yes, we were now even and the score had been settled, but unfortunately the officers with me didn't give me a chance to explain. It all got out of hand when one of them thought it would be a good idea to get their taser out." Barksley said before stopping. Turning his attention to the teapot once more, checking it had brewed enough, he started pouring out the cups of tea, then adding the milk. "So I went back to the station to sort out the details. No charges have been pressed and I hope we can now be friends once more."

Barksley handed George a cup of tea as a symbol of their new allegiance. George took the tea and nodded his head in agreement. Barksley then handed out the tea cups to the rest of the room.

"Right, now that's out the way... what the hell has been going on here?" Barksley asked the rest of the gathered crowd.

They talked about the secret rooms under the library and Alan's misadventure with the pickaxe bringing the ceiling down. Officers had been into the passageway and down the spiral staircase, but it was completely blocked at the bottom.

There was no sign of Alan, it had been presumed that the rubble pile contained his remains. A specialist excavation team was on its way to clear the room and make it safe. George complained in jest about the peace and quiet of his home being ruined with all the people milling about, as well as the vans and their flashing lights outside.

Once Barksley was satisfied with the report, he collected up the empty teacups and told them all to go home. He saw David get up gingerly from the armchair and insisted on dropping Evelyn and David home after the misunderstanding from earlier that morning.

EPILOGUE

David got out of the police car gingerly and shut the door behind him. Barksley put the police car in gear, wheel spinning away.

David walked slowly up the driveway back to his house and retrieved the new key from his jacket pocket. Barksley had handed it to him before he got out the car, saying it had taken him a while to find where Officer Smith had run off to, so he could get the new key the locksmith had provided. Barksley finally found Smith huddled at the back of one of the police vans, cowering under a blanket.

David unlocked the front door with his new key, walked in and shut the door behind him, ensuring the newly added deadbolt was locked tight.

He sat on his sofa and put his feet up, shoes and uniform still on, and fell immediately asleep.

He shot awake, a loud rattling noise awakening him. Someone was trying to open the front door, but the new deadbolt held firm. The noise stopped for a few moments. David got himself up from his chair and headed slowly to the door, trying to be as quiet as possible.

He saw the letter box hinge upwards and a gloved hand stretch through, reaching towards the lock. The hand couldn't reach the lock so it retreated back out, lowering the hinged letterbox cover back down slowly.

David took a deep breath, calming his nerves. He knew what he had to do.

He unlocked the deadbolt and slowly swung the door open.

"I want the ring!" came a gravelly voice from a dark silhouetted figure in the doorway.

"Ok. I'll get it now." David said calmly. He started for his left pocket, before a thought came to his groggy mind, the adrenaline pumping around his body making him more and more awake by the moment.

Instead he went for his right jacket pocket, but he felt for something other than the ring. Finding what he was looking for, he slowly pulled his hand out of his pocket until it was almost fully free of the jacket. Then he sped up, quickly raising his right hand with its contents.

Aiming and pressing the trigger to the taser instantly before the character dressed in black could react. 50,000 volts shot through the wires, incapacitating the victim. They fell to the ground in an undignified heap.

David was now glad that Barksley had insisted he take the taser along with the new key to his house.

"This isn't over!" The gravelly deep voice threatened in a quiet whisper before going completely silent.

ABOUT THE AUTHOR

C. S. Rhymes

C.S. Rhymes is a full time web developer and a part time author, living in the United Kingdom.

He wrote his first book called "How NOT to make a website" that's designed for business owners and website owners to help them understand what NOT to do when making their website.

He was looking at the books on the Kindle Store and noticed that many of them had very similar titles, such as "10 ways to promote your site", or "Easy ways of getting to the top of search engines". This got him thinking about the many common mistakes that people make when designing, building and editing their website and it gave him an idea to confront this from a different angle. This lead him to write a book about how not to make a website, to help you understand what to avoid when making a site to help improve your visitors experience.

He has also written another book in the series,

called "How NOT to use a smartphone" to help beginners to smartphones jump from their feature phone to a smartphone.

Not satisfied with writing non-fiction, C.S. Rhymes turned his attention to writing his first fiction story, called "Nigel's Intranet Adventure". The story follows an IT worker, stuck in the day to day of office life, when a chance encounter with a new employee turns his life upside down.

C.S. Rhymes is now writing a new crime mystery series, "The Little-Astwick Mysteries", with the first in the series "Trouble at the church" available on Kindle and paperback now.

As well as full blown books, he is also keen on writing short stories. A collection of short stories called "Unlooked for Tales", was released on ebook in 2024.

BOOKS BY THIS AUTHOR

How Not To Make A Website

What I have learnt from over twelve years' experience of working on websites is that there are many things to avoid when making your website, in a sense, I have learnt How NOT to make a website.

I want you to succeed by sharing my knowledge and experience to help you avoid some of the basic mistakes when creating your website to create a better user experience for your visitors, as well as making life easier for you by reducing unnecessary maintenance.

How Not To Use A Smartphone

This book is written for all those people that over the years have shied away from getting a smartphone in the past and their old trusty Nokia 3310 has finally beeped its last polyphonic ringtone.

It's designed to give you a head start into the world of smartphones, by helping you understand "How NOT to use a smartphone" so that you can tell your swipe from your pinch and zoom.

Nigel's Intranet Adventure

Follow Nigel on an adventure that would change his life forever, all triggered by a chance encounter with a new starter at work (Dave), that throws his safe and consistent, but insanely boring, world into chaos, which quickly transforms into a new found friendship and a leads to a journey of technological invention, trickery and wonder.

The Little-Astwick Mysteries - Trouble At The Church

A fast paced crime mystery set in the fictional English village of Little-Astwick.

Follow David Morgan, a Community Support Officer, new to the area, as he gets plunged in at the deep end with a new acquaintance, Evelyn McKenzie, trying to figure out what has been going on at the village church.

Whilst out walking her faithful dog, (Charlie), Evelyn noticed the church doors were open and signs of a disturbance inside.

Accompany the duo through their investigation around the village, in their attempts to solve the mystery of Little-Astwick.

Unlooked For Tales

A collection of short stories describing everyday events in life that aren't always so everyday.

Sometimes you need to stop, take a breath and look around you and appreciate the moment, as it won't be there again.

Thinking back or ahead, you may have a set of milestone events in your life, but sometimes the events that stick with you the most are unplanned, or even unlooked for.